LOVE AND MURDER ON THE HILL

CATHERINE ANGELONE

iUniverse, Inc.
Bloomington

Love and Murder on the Hill

Copyright © 2011 Catherine Angelone

All rights reserved. No part of this book may be used or reproduced by any means, graphic, electronic, or mechanical, including photocopying, recording, taping or by any information storage retrieval system without the written permission of the publisher except in the case of brief quotations embodied in critical articles and reviews.

This is a work of fiction. All of the characters, names, incidents, organizations, and dialogue in this novel are either the products of the author's imagination or are used fictitiously.

iUniverse books may be ordered through booksellers or by contacting:

iUniverse
1663 Liberty Drive
Bloomington, IN 47403
www.iuniverse.com
1-800-Authors (1-800-288-4677)

Because of the dynamic nature of the Internet, any web addresses or links contained in this book may have changed since publication and may no longer be valid. The views expressed in this work are solely those of the author and do not necessarily reflect the views of the publisher, and the publisher hereby disclaims any responsibility for them.

Any people depicted in stock imagery provided by Thinkstock are models, and such images are being used for illustrative purposes only.

Certain stock imagery © Thinkstock.

ISBN: 978-1-4620-0083-8 (pbk)
ISBN: 978-1-4620-0084-5 (clth)
ISBN: 978-1-4620-0085-2 (pbk)

Library of Congress Control Number: 2011903060

Printed in the United States of America

iUniverse rev. date: 3/9/11

I dedicate this book to
my sister Darlene Jackson
You've come a long way baby!
Keep up the good work!

I would like to include
In this dedication a wonderful
friend, Laura Singer from Brooklyn NY.
What can I say? You rock girl!
Thanks for all your help and input.

To my niece Sarah Buscumb
www.mobilehairstylists.com
Thanks for making me look natural
And not as if I was going to a prom.

ONE

"I was just walking along the river's edge when I came across the body," the old man said as he wiped the perspiration from his brow. He removed his light jacket and revealed a weathered grey shirt that was damp from sweat.

He took off his baseball cap, tucked his thick grey hair back behind his ears, and placed the cap back on his head. "That's when I called you fellows to report it."

"Do you always walk along here so early in the morning?" Detective Sarah Child asked.

"Every morning," he said without conviction." It keeps me in shape, and it's good for my dog Piper."

A small terrier, with matching grey hair, lay at his feet, oblivious to the detective.

"Did you notice anything unusual, like a stranger in the area?"

"A part from this dead woman, nothing."

"If you have time to come down to the station we could have one of the officers take down a formal statement from you."

The old man nodded and made a promise to do that first thing this afternoon.

"Come on Piper," the man said, tugging on the leash. The dog yawned and dragged his tired body to his feet and slowly followed his master.

"What do we have?" a voice asked Sarah. She turned and flashed a smile at her partner, Charles Richmond, who was making his way over to the crime scene.

She handed him a pair of latex gloves which he immediately slipped on. "From what I can see, it could be an accidental drowning, but I won't know anything positive until we get the medical examiner to look at her."

Charles lifted the blue plastic cover that was placed over the body to shield it from the already forming crowd of tourists and locals. He examined the body briefly as the men from the coroner's office made their way down the Hill to remove the body.

A few uniformed officers were ordering the ever growing crowd to stay behind the yellow tape that was placed along the railing that separated the road and the Hill.

"Do you think it's another victim from the same killer?" he asked Sarah.

She was busy directing the police photographer while marking possible evidence. "The body was found in the same way as the other two, but we won't be sure until the coroner takes a look. It could possibly be a simple drowning."

"Let's just hope we don't have any connection," he said.

Sarah glanced over and couldn't help but notice the worried look on her partner's face. She was feeling the same thing when the call came.

The body was found on the shore of the Niagara River, less than a mile down from where the first body was found. The second body was found floating on the United States side of the river. No connection was made with the first body until they found out she was a missing Canadian woman.

The connection was made further when they discovered that the body had the same ligatures on the ankles and wrists. Just like the first two victims, this body was of a young woman, possibly in her late teens, early twenties.

The first two bodies showed they died from asphyxiation. There was duct tape residue found around the victims' mouth and nose.

There were remnants of a plastic bag as well as the duct tape residue around the neck of each victim. This indicated that not only were the victims' mouths and noses taped, but the killer may have taken the extra measure by taping some sort of plastic hood or bag over the victims' head to cut off any air.

Both victims were sexually assaulted, and there were fibers of some type of nylon cord found on the tape residue as well as their clothing. The cords may have been removed before they were thrown into the river. All the bodies were dead before being put in the water.

Charles took one more look at the body, paying closer attention to the arms and legs. He shook his head in disbelief, when he noticed the red and purple marks on the body's wrists and ankles.

Charles had worked the beat in the roughest part of Toronto. After working homicide in the big city for five years, he felt himself becoming numb to anything in his life. He was losing touch with reality and needed to slow his pace down. He put in for a transfer to the Niagara Police Department, and they jumped at the chance to have him on board. After six months working at a slower and less traumatic pace, he was staring down at the third body in three months.

He left Toronto to get away from all the violence and killings he'd seen. He knew that he'd eventually be involved with murder and death in the area, but he thought it would be some time before he would have to encounter a murder, let alone a possible serial killer.

The body was bagged and loaded into the coroners van. The crowd slowly thinned out as the body was driven to the coroner's office for further examination. Only a few uniformed officers, a small handful of detectives as well as Charles and Sarah were left to go over the site.

Charles broke off from the group and walked up the shore of the river looking for anything unusual. He figured the body washed ashore where it was found, so this meant it was dumped somewhere up river.

There was the possibility that it was dumped above the falls but for it to arrive at its final destination, it would have to be dumped close to the falls' edge. That would have been nearly impossible without being seen. Even farther up before the falls would have been even more difficult.

There were places someone could have disposed of the body farther up before the falls but there were several small islands as well as rocks that would have snagged the body before it reached the falls edge.

He watched the Maid of the Mist make its voyage up the river toward the falls. It stopped briefly in the middle of the whirlpool as tourists clad in blue raincoats took pictures of the surrounding area.

Charles continued his way up the river until he was out of view from the cameras of the boat. The area that the body was found wasn't well traveled by tourists. If the body had indeed been dumped where it was found, then it only left to reason that the killer had to be local. If someone didn't know this area of the river one could easily slip into the water and be dragged down with the undertow.

Charles took care as to stay far enough from the edge of the river. He looked for any sign of disturbance, such as a footprint in the mud or an indication that something was dragged to the water. He watched the movement of the current. His eyes followed the moving water to see if it ended at the place where the body was found.

"This is hopeless," he mumbled to himself. "It's like finding a needle in a haystack."

He was about to give up when something caught his eye. He moved closer to the shiny object protruding out of the mud. It was too close to the water's edge, so he used a long stick to try and retrieve it from the constantly wet ground. After a few tries, he was able to scrape it close enough so he could reach over and remove it from the mud.

He used some of his bottled water to wash away enough of the mud to reveal a woman's silver pendant with the initial 'J' outlined with rhinestones. Some of the rhinestones were missing.

Charles placed the necklace in a plastic bag and shoved it in his pocket. He looked around the area and noticed a slightly overgrown path that led to a hidden area of the road above.

Maybe the killer brought the body down that path, he thought. He may have placed the body to look like it was washed ashore.

He made note of some freshly broken branches along the base of the path.

Charles waved to Sarah, who was talking to a couple of officers. She walked down the river's edge and joined Charles near the path.

He pulled the bagged necklace out of his pocket. "I found this necklace over at the edge," he said, pointing to the spot in the mud.

Sarah examined the area, careful not to step too close. She looked up at the path. "I doubt if our killer would have used this path to dump the body," Sarah said.

"It's just a thought," Charles replied. "Let's get a better look at the path."

They slowly made their way up the path, examining the area for fresh footprints. They had an unusually dry spring, making the ground hard. No footprints were evident in the ground. The farther they went up the path, the steeper it became. By the time they reached the top they were practically on their hands and knees climbing the side of the Hill.

"I don't remember it ever being this steep." Sarah said as she hoisted herself over the guard rail and dusted the knees of her navy suit free from dirt.

Charles joined her on the other side of the railing and pulled prickers off his black suit pants. "You've been down that path before?"

"As a teenager a bunch of us used to go down there to drink beer and smoke cigarettes that someone would steal from their parents. Sometimes we would pay someone's older brother to buy us the stuff. I guess being young and foolish, you don't realize the danger involved in doing those things."

"I would never have thought of you as the wild and crazy type."

"You'd be surprised at what I was capable of doing back then." She grinned, tossing her red hair back seductively.

Charles was tempted to ask more, but decided otherwise.

Although Sarah was attractive and single, Charles had labeled her *hands off*. Charles always made it a point to not get involved in any office romance. Sarah was his partner at work, and he didn't want their relationship to be anything but professional.

Sarah, on the other hand, was smitten with her new partner. He's handsome and blond and knew his work. He filled out a pair of jeans in all the right places, and had eyes the color of aqua blue. She had subtly thrown herself at him on numerous occasions without success.

When it came to his personal life, Charles was mum on the subject. The only thing she did know about him was that he never married and was in between girlfriends. That was about the extent of information he'd given her. She was tempted to find out more through other means but figured he'd tell her everything in his own time.

She just wished he'd sometime ask her out for dinner that didn't consist of a quick hamburger at a fast food joint while talking shop. Or at the very least welcome her advances instead of playing dumb.

"I'm going to head back to the office to check out any missing persons," Charles said as they walked to his car.

"I still have a few things to do here," Sarah replied.

"Want to get together tonight for a bite to eat?" She silently bit her tongue as she realized what she said.

Charles thought for a moment then smiled. "I might take you up on the offer, but it would depend on what's waiting for me back at the office."

He wrapped his arm around Sarah's shoulder and gave her a brotherly squeeze.

His touch made her feel warm and fuzzy all over. She wanted to grab his face and kiss him, but held back. Too much too fast, she thought. I'll get him drunk first before I do that.

TWO

"So what do you say we catch a late supper tonight?" Marco asked as he sat himself down in Grace's clients' chair.

He was dressed in his usual wife beaters shirt and camel toe forming jeans. He topped off his look with tacky gold chains and drug store sunglasses. He hadn't changed his look much since the early nineties but his attire seemed more in fitting with the eighties.

Grace's oversized jewelry clinked as she gathered up her cards and closed up shop for the night. "I told you I won't go out with you."

Marco blew out a sigh and leaned back in the chair. "What will it take to change your mind?"

"A lobotomy comes to mind, as well as memory erasing if there is such a thing."

Marco thought for a moment. "I don't think there's such a thing, and come to think of it, I doubt if they perform lobotomies anymore."

She pulled her umbrella out of the table and laid it on the ground, glancing over at Marco Ciccerelli, who was grinning ear to ear like a wolf waiting to devour a defenseless lamb.

Grace shook her head and a shudder left her lips as she tried to get the image of the two of them together, out of her mind.

"You have a better chance of white elephants flying out your ass, Marco, before I'd ever consider going out on a date with you."

Marco's eyes widened, and for a brief moment Grace thought she'd seen his frosted white tips turn red. Then she realized it was the lighting from the Castle Restaurant's neon sign.

Marco was a womanizer as far as the eye could see. He hit on every female who walked by, trying to entice them to try his game. He was good at the talk, and he walked the walk. But he was far from Grace's type.

Any woman with half a brain wasn't Marco's type. He preferred them busty, young, and dumb as a box of hair. The complete opposite of Grace.

Every summer he scored with the young tourists who flocked Clifton Hill. Most were barely drinking age, and they were blown over by Marco's good looks and rock hard body. They swallowed up every one of his pick up lines and were eager to see him again.

But Marco had one rule he lived by. One date, one lay. Unless, of course, the girl was exceptionally good between the sheets, then he might consider a second date. But the majority would come back the next day, and Marco would blow them off, saying he was busy working and that he'd call them.

He never did call, and they left with a broken heart or would turn their advances toward his partner Aaron who quickly brushed them off.

At first Grace found it amusing. She'd watch Marco break into a sweat when last night's date would show up, but then it became sad. Some of the girls would make scenes by crying and screaming.

This made it difficult for Marco, but even more difficult for Grace to concentrate on her readings. Even Aaron Stein, who worked the rock climbing wall, was getting peeved at Marco's behavior.

They'd been friends since childhood and went into business together, opening the wall and bell games and making a pretty decent living at it. Unfortunately, according to Aaron, Marco spent money faster than he made it. Still, they remained friends, and for some reason the business survived.

Grace knew both of them growing up. They were part of the gang of kids who used her for target practice by throwing rocks at her. Grace cringed when they opened up across the alley from her, but soon she was okay with it. Aaron had turned into a somewhat decent human being, in spite of taking Marco on as a partner.

He was actually nice to her, and it was obvious that he had matured and left his rock throwing ways behind him. But Grace still kept the friendship with both men at arm's length. It wasn't as easy for her to put the past behind.

Grace got everything in the trunk and called it a night. She waved to Jim, the motel manager, as she inched her way out of the parking lot into oncoming traffic that lined Clifton Hill.

It was just past eight and the neon lights blared brightly along the Hill as Graced moved at a snail's pace up the street towards Lundy's Lane.

Her stomach growled, and it suddenly hit Grace she hadn't eaten since lunch.

In less than an hour the fireworks would begin at the Falls and Grace didn't dare turn around for fear of getting trapped on the Hill, so she decided to find a restaurant closer to home.

Ten minutes later Grace was standing at the counter of the flying saucer restaurant on Lundy's Lane ordering a turkey sub to go.

Nothing changed with the Flying Saucer Restaurant. It was still in the shape of a round space ship painted in faded metallic grey and mauve paint. The architecture was out of place with all the more modern stores that lined Lundy's Lane, especially since it sat farther up in the less touristy area.

The interior didn't fare any better with its hard molded booths and worn sixties tables. Each booth seat was molded with a different color. Orange, mauve, yellow and green were the standard colors.

The other thing that never changed was their great food. Although the restaurant had changed hands over the years and the prices increased with the cost of living since they first opened, they were still without a doubt the best subs in town. Maybe even in the world.

Not that Grace was an authority on subs from around the world. All she knew was that if you wanted a good turkey sub you had to go to the Flying Saucer.

Grace was tired, and wanted to eat lying down in front of her television. Pathetic, she knew, but it beat sitting alone in one of those hard booths until her butt went numb.

Twenty minutes later Grace was free of her heavy makeup and jewelry and replaced her gypsy attire for flannel pajamas. She channel surfed for something good to watch, finally settling on a South Park rerun. She needed a good laugh after a long day.

Just as Grace was beginning to unwind, a knock came at her back door. Just what I need, company, she thought.

Grace used to live with her grandmother and mother but when she returned from university, they felt Grace needed her own space. Grace felt the same way. When her mother and grandmother expanded the downstairs, they added a small two bedroom second floor apartment on the back of the house with a separate entrance. This was where Grace called home. But it still was close enough to her family.

Her furniture was used and overstuffed. Her kitchen table was wood veneer with mismatched chairs. Her television was the latest flat screen with sound surround and blueray video. This was Grace to a tee. Everything in the apartment suited her.

Grace sighed as she walked to the back door and saw her grandmother and mother waving through the glass window.

"Did you hear about the body they found by the Niagara River?" Granny asked as Grace let the women in.

"I just got home."

"It's all over the news," her mother continued. "We thought we could do a séance to see if we can get any information from the spirits. You know how easy it is for a spirit to take over your body than me and your grandmother."

Grace gave out a yawn. "If it's all the same to the two of you, I'll pass on it tonight. I've had a long day, and my mind is drained. The last thing I want to do is go downstairs and sit in a circle waiting for the spirits to contact us and take over my body. Besides, I'm sure the spirits won't mind if I sit this one out."

Granny handed Grace a plate of her special white chocolate chip cookies. "I baked these today and saved you a plate." She kissed Grace on the forehead. "If you change your mind, you know where we are."

She hugged them both and watched them scurry down the stairs like two little mice, and disappear inside the back door of the house. Grace closed and locked the door and took the cookies into the living room. Granny always had perfect timing. She must have known that Grace needed some of her cookies to end her day.

Charles sat at his desk looking over the evidence of the two previous murders. A peg board with photos and information on the first two victims lined the wall behind his heavy oak desk. A vacant area was reserved for the report on today's body.

Sarah stood in the doorway, watching her partner. "You look deep in thought."

Charles swivelled his chair in her direction. "I didn't know you were there," he said, startled by her presence.

Sarah moved into the office and closed the door behind her. She took a seat across from Charles and watched in silence as he studied the photos and read the information for each victim.

"Melanie Thompson, age twenty-one, was the first victim," Charles read aloud. "Do we have information on her?" he asked.

Sarah moved next to Charles. "Nothing as of yet."

Their attention moved to the next victim.

"Lydia Mac Donald, age nineteen," Sarah read. "She's the one who was found on the States side."

Charles sighed. "Do you see any connections between these two victims aside from the evident?"

"So far all we have is they are both from the surrounding area, young and pretty. We tried finding a connection such as mutual friends or jobs, but we drew a blank," Sarah said.

"Once we have and identification on this new body hopefully she will hold some connection to one of the other victims," Charles added.

"I gather by your words you think she's victim number three?" Sarah asked.

Charles nodded. "I have no doubt about it. I saw the same marks on her as on the other two. This'll be victim three and if we don't get some break in this case soon, there might be a victim four."

Sarah nodded without saying a word.

They stood for a moment in silence as concern filled their thoughts.

Charles stretched out his arms, and rubbed his eyes. "What time is it?" He yawned.

"It's past midnight, and we should be in bed."

Charles glanced sideways at his partner, and smiled.

Sarah felt heat rise from beneath her white dress shirt and stop short of her forehead, realizing what she said. "I don't mean together. Um, err. I meant that."

Charles laughed. "I know what you meant, Sarah. Relax."

She sighed with relief.

Charles made her feel awkward with his good looks and sophisticated charm. He probably made all women feel awkward, Sarah thought. He carried himself as if he graduated with straight A's from Charm School. He looked good in anything that he chose to wear.

Charles seemed worldly even though she knew very little about him. She felt he was way out of her league, but she still had visions of the two of them together on a more intimate setting.

"Come on. It's time to close up shop," he said as he pushed his partner out the door.

"I hope that we can catch this guy before he strikes again," Charles said as they walked through the small parking lot toward their cars.

"It's a long weekend, and the people are already starting to come over the border in droves. The last thing we need is to announce a serial killer on the loose.

"Maybe we should start talking to some of the locals who run the stores and tourist areas of Clifton Hill?" Charles suggested.

"It wouldn't hurt but the people on the Hill are pretty tight lipped when it comes to talking about each other, especially to the police," Sarah said. "They barely talk to me and I grew up with most of them. I don't see them being open to a total stranger like you."

Charles held the car door open for Sarah. "I guess we'll have to find a way to reach out to some of them for help."

A thought came to Sarah. "You know, we could always seek the help of our local fortune tellers to give us a hand.

Charles closed the car door. "Are you joking?"

"You never know. I went to school with Grace Bardo. Her mother and grandmother are mediums and fortune tellers. I used to hear my mother talk about how accurate they were. But I had my own experience with them when I was eight."

Charles wasn't sure if Sarah was being serious or sarcastic.

He believed in the supernatural world. Maybe not to the extent as others, but he did feel there was some truth to it.

She could tell by the look on Charles' face he was mulling it over.

Sarah gave out a laugh. "Don't tell me you're thinking about it?"

"It wouldn't hurt to check it out."

She shook her head in disbelief. "I was only joking, but if you do, count me out. Those women freaked me out when I was young. When we moved to the area, and I had to switch schools, I met Grace and became friends with her."

Sarah gave Charles the short version of how she was scared out of her wits by the séance she was forced to participate with the night she slept over at their house.

"Sounds like it would've been fun." Charles grinned.

"Maybe now it would be. But when you're eight years old, it was no picnic. I had nightmares for a week after that."

"Sounds like an interesting family."

Sarah shrugged her shoulders and started her car. "I can't believe I mentioned this to you. And I can't believe you're actually thinking of contacting them."

"Do you think they're still around?" he asked.

She was at a loss for words. She only mentioned it as a joke, and he was taking it seriously. "I would never have taken you for one to believe in that stuff, but if you really want to do this, just don't mention my name, okay?"

Charles gave his partner a salute. "Will do," he said, snapping to attention.

Sarah wasn't amused. "They live on Lundy's Lane. You'll find them there. You can't miss the place. It's the only pink stucco building on the street.

The last I heard Grace went off to university. Not sure what she's doing now, but I'm sure her mother and crazy grandmother can help you out."

Sarah backed out of her parking spot and put the car in drive. "Come to think of it, you could even try down the alley off of the Hill. Her mother used to do readings for the tourists during the summer. She might still be there," she said before driving away.

Sarah waved as she pulled out of the parking lot and disappeared into the traffic.

Charles got into his car and headed in the direction of Lundy's Lane.

The traffic was still heavy as Charles passed Clifton Hill. He gritted his teeth as he inched his car forward, finally making it through the light. "I left Toronto to get out of this kind of traffic," he said under his breath. "Doesn't anyone ever sleep anymore?"

The tourist area of the Falls was lit up with neon signs and flashing lights. Some shops were closed for the night except for a few souvenir shops, the haunted house and the pubs that lined Clifton Hill and Lundy's Lane.

He hit the brakes as a young couple dodged traffic to cross the street against the light.

"Hey! You're crossing against the light! Don't you know what you did is illegal and you can get ticketed for it?" he shouted out the window at the people.

"So what? Pedestrians have the right away!" the guy yelled back.

"Not when you're crossing against the light, you moron!"

The guy flipped Charles the bird. "So what? You a cop?"

Charles was tired and had enough with seeing tourists in the area disrespecting the rules. Whatever his reasons for feeling the way he did, he needed to set an example to everyone else. Or at the very least embarrass the shit out of the guy in front of his girlfriend.

He pulled his car over and put on the police lights inside his car.

The couple froze in their place, and the color drained from their face.

"As a matter of fact, I am," Charles said as he walked over to the couple.

"Um, I'm sorry, officer. I didn't mean anything by it," the young man said.

His girlfriend punched him in the arm. "I told you we shouldn't have crossed, but no! You had to be the macho man and drag me through the traffic."

Charles hadn't been in Niagara Falls for long before he was called to the tourist area because some person decided to do the exact same thing as this couple. It seemed that every holiday someone would get hit by a car because they refused to follow the rules.

"I'll let the two of you off with a warning. But if I ever catch you doing that again, I'll fine you, and it'll be a hefty one," he said sternly.

"Thank you, officer," the woman said. "It won't happen again."

Charles climbed back into his car, inched back into traffic, and flipped his lights off. "What the hell did I just do? I must be getting nasty in my old age."

The traffic started to thin out as he drove up Lundy's Lane toward the edge of town. The motels and tourist traps were replaced with pharmacies and grocery stores. As he neared the end of the tourist shops, he noticed the pink house with the fortune telling sign. It was tucked away on a corner lot facing Lundy's Lane. He turned down the small side street and wheeled into the back parking lot to turn around.

There were no lights on; except for neon sign reading <u>closed</u> which shone brightly in the back window. There was an identical sign in the front window. The parking lot was empty except for two cars. Must belong to the apartment upstairs and the owners, he thought.

Charles got out of his car and walked around the front of the building to check out the hours of operation. It was past one in the morning and to find anyone up at that time was near to impossible.

He walked back to his car and noticed a light on in the upstairs back window. Maybe someone is up after all, he thought. But then again, maybe the person who lives there isn't associated with the store on the main floor.

He decided to come back first thing in the morning.

THREE

Grace was jolted awake with the feeling of falling. She'd passed out on the sofa, and her body was stiff from not moving for over an hour. The television was playing David Letterman as Grace pulled her tired body off the sofa. She flipped the TV off and noted the time on her watch. It was just past one.

Grace heard the sound of a car starting and the flash of headlights in her kitchen window. She peeked out the window in her bedroom just in time to see a car pull out of the parking lot. Probably someone turning around, she thought.

It happened a lot during tourist season. Most would travel up Lundy's Lane until they realized they were out of the tourist section.

Some would be curious about the shop and pull in to take a look. Others would be in search of something a little more erotic and go to the adult store next door. And some would keep going to the outskirts of town where the local strip clubs were situated.

Grace had that sneaky suspicion that this was more than a case of a lost tourist. She gave her body a shake as she tried to dismiss the feelings and chalked it up to sleeping on the sofa.

Grace opened her eyes to the sound of rain hitting her bedroom window. Overnight the sky turned steel grey, and the air went from sticky hot and sunny to bone-chilling rain. This was more in keeping with the usual May weather. One day could be beautiful, the next day cold rain.

"No point in opening shop today," Grace mumbled as she pulled the blankets around her shoulders, and buried her face in the pillow.

Grace felt herself drifting back to sleep, but suddenly jolted awake by the sound of the phone.

"Are you coming down for breakfast?" Mom asked on the other end of the line.

Grace mumbled something that sounded like a cross between yes and what the hell.

Grace hated to cook, even if cooking consisted of toasting bread. She knew if she refused, she'd be out breakfast. "Give me five minutes," Grace said before hanging up.

Grace dragged her tired body out of bed and headed for the bathroom. She flipped on the shower, brushed her teeth, then stood in the hot shower, letting the water do its job of waking her up.

Grace dried herself off and wrapped her thick long black hair in a towel. She slipped on a pair of black sweatpants and matching hoodie and hurried down the back steps of the building. The smell of breakfast filled her senses as she joined her family in the kitchen in the back of the main floor.

"You'll catch your death of cold going out with wet hair," Granny said.

"I have it wrapped in a towel."

"Still, you shouldn't be going out with wet hair," she scolded.

Grace did an eye roll and dug into the plate of scrambled eggs her mother set in front of her.

Mom and granny took their place at the table.

"Before I forget, Margaret Summers called and asked if you can drive the twins to work this morning. I told her that you wouldn't mind," mom said.

"What time do they need to be there?"

"Around eleven or so."

Grace nodded while continuing to shovel eggs and bacon in her mouth.

"Should we tell her?" Granny asked mom.

Grace looked up from her plate. "Tell me what?"

Usually when they open a conversation with *should we tell her*, it's almost never good news for Grace.

Grace was raised by her mother and grandmother. As far back as she can remember no men lived under their roof.

With the exception of her great grandfather Paul.

Love and Murder on the Hill

According to Grace's grandmother, her great grandparents fled Hungary during the Second World War when gypsies were being rounded up for extermination. They eventually made their way to Niagara Falls, Canada, bringing with them one suitcase, their baby daughter, and their gypsy ways.

What her great grandfather Paul lacked in labor skills, he made up in fighting and conning. He was the epitome of tall, dark, and handsome and spent his free time chasing any skirt that ventured by.

Because of his distaste for manual labor and his inability to stay with one job more than a week, he had plenty of free time on his hands to pursue his love for women.

He would take any odd job that would come his way, make enough money to buy himself into a drunken stupor, and look for the biggest guy to pick a fight with. This usually followed with Paul getting his ass kicked and thrown out on the street.

The police would be called and Paul would be picked up off the street by the officers on call and brought back to Helga, who would nurse him back to health.

This ritual was played out at least twice a month.

Unfortunately, Helga turned a blind eye to his fighting and flirting ways.

From the bits and pieces that Grace gathered from her grandmother, Helga had secretly hoped that a new start in a new country would encourage her husband to settle down and try to build a stable life for his family, but nothing had changed.

He still insisted that he was destined for greater things. The only thing that Paul was actually good at was getting into fights, drinking, and making love. Not necessarily in that order.

Because of the lack of money coming into the home, Helga would take in ironing from the local hotels and restaurants. But this was hard work, long hours, and barely enough to pay the rent, let alone put food on the table.

Back in Hungary, Helga's specialty was fortune telling. Their caravan moved from town to town and entertained the locals.

She'd have a little tent set up to allow private readings for anyone who wanted to know their future. Because of the lack of money she decided to open shop in their small one bedroom apartment on Lundy's lane. It was the one thing she knew and was good at.

Helga wasn't just a regular run of the mill fortune teller who would tell you what you wanted to hear just so you would come back to spend more money. She was the real deal. She was accurate in everything she said, and she held nothing back, even if it meant bad news. Her honesty and uncanny ability became well known in the area, and it made her a nice living to support her family.

Because of her husband's squandering of any money he made, Helga was careful to hide her business affairs from him. She was able to arrange a barter system with many of the local merchants. This allowed her to always have food on the table and clothes on their backs as well as make the payments for their monthly bills.

This gift was handed down to her through the centuries and just like Helga, her daughter inherited the ability.

In other families, children would be born with the same nose or unusual colored eyes.

In Grace's family it was the gift as her grandmother called it. The gift was the ability to tell the future and speak with spirits. The first born female was destined to use her gift to help others and it didn't hurt to make a few bucks along the way.

They sat silent with grins that had trouble written all over their faces.

"Okay. Spill it," Grace demanded.

Mom and granny moved closer to Grace as if they were afraid anyone else was going to hear them.

"It seems that the spirits were talking about you last night," Mom said. "Something is going to happen, and you're going to meet someone who will have a big impact in your life."

Granny nodded in agreement. "We were also told to watch for a car that will be bringing this person to you."

Seeing that everyone and their dog owned a car in Niagara Falls, Grace didn't put too much faith in what the spirits had to say on this matter.

Grace glanced from her mom to her granny and back again. Her mouth was open as she listened to their news.

"Maybe it was the car I saw in the parking lot last night," Grace said after which seemed like ten minutes.

They looked at each other. "Oh, this is great news!" Granny squealed with delight. "Maybe this is the person whom the spirits talked about."

"But then again it could have been another lost tourist," Grace added.

Love and Murder on the Hill

The spirits were grasping at straws, Grace thought.
Any talk of a man entering her life spelled trouble.

Just like her grandmother, her mother never married. They were guided to the future father of their first born, by the spirits. This was the only way to ensure that their child would be a girl and would be born with the gift.

Grace never knew her father, and her mother never talked about him. The only information Grace had was he was from Italy. Her mother met him while he was vacationing in the city with his wife and kids. That might explain Grace's love for pizza and all things Italian.

That was the extent of any knowledge of him. For a while when she was young, she thought her thick black hair was her inheritance from her father. But family photos put an end to that thought, as all the women had the same hair. Granny's hair was still thick but went from jet black to steel grey. Her mother's was on the road to looking the same.

Graces' mother's father was French Canadian and lived in Quebec. She wasn't even sure if he was still alive or if he even knew he had a daughter, let alone a granddaughter. Either way, her family never talked about them and their names were never mentioned. Not that Grace would know their names anyway.

The front door buzzer went off.
"Customer," Grace said to get their minds off of her life and any stranger who'd be entering it.
Mom checked her watch. "They're coming in early," she said as she noted the time. "I haven't even changed into my black dress."
Graces' mother and grandmother always like to dress like gypsies when greeting customers. It made their shop look more authentic. Grace too enjoyed dressing up in a peasant type outfit with flowing skirt, white puffed blouse and heavy makeup.

It drew people to her like a magnet. It didn't hurt that she would show a little cleavage with each outfit. Not that she had that much cleavage to show.

In food terms Grace's breast size fell between eggs and tangerines. She thanked Victoria secret and their miracle push-up bra for making them look more like round Macintosh apples.

When she wasn't working on the Hill, she'd opt for tees and jeans with minimal makeup which was a far cry from her brightly colored working clothes.

The women hurried through the door that separated their living quarters from the store, leaving Grace to her thoughts and her scrambled eggs. Grace sipped her tea as she listened to the women chat away with a man about their business.

"The person you'd want to speak with is my daughter," Mom said to the stranger.

"I'll get her," Granny said. She stuck her head in the kitchen doorway. "Grace, can you come out here for a minute? There's someone in need of your services."

Grace sighed deeply, dragged her ass off the kitchen chair, and followed her grandmother into the front of the store.

The outside of the store was pink stucco but the inside was dark and mysterious. On one wall there were candles in every color for every occasion. Each had a specific purpose. Instructions were neatly typed and taped to the candles to ensure their used properly.

A large counter held charms and stones. All the stones are cleansed and blessed before purchase so no negative energy will follow the buyer.

The charms are made by a local silversmith. Granny would give him specific instructions on the design and he'd create the design to every detail.

People would buy them, not for their special abilities, but for the workmanship and the originality of each design. They're the biggest seller in the entire shop.

Behind the counter stood a heavy wooden bookshelf with pull out drawers. Granny salvaged it from the old library when it was being replaced with a more modern yet sterile glass and concrete library.

Each drawer was catalogued with special herbs for potions. Jars filled with dried flowers, vegetables and herbs lined the bottom shelves.

She stopped in her tracks at the sight of the tall, handsome stranger who stood before her.

Grace has an uncanny ability to see auras, and his was the brightest she'd ever seen. His eyes were the bluest she had ever seen, too.

His blond hair was thick and wavy and was slicked back to make him appear older and more professional. But it couldn't take away from his boyish good looks. He looked like Daniel Craig as James Bond. Grace loved those Bond movies.

A smiled filled his face and showed dimples that made Grace's heart skip a beat. She felt her stomach do a flip and land just above her hoohaa.

He extended his hand to Grace. "Hi, I'm Charles. I hope they didn't get you out of the shower to meet me," he said.

Grace gave him a puzzled look until she realized she still had her hair wrapped in a towel. "Um no, no. I um always wear my hair like this on Saturday's." Grace gave herself a mental slap on the forehead for her stupid remark.

She pulled the towel off her head and let her long black hair fall freely down her back. Grace tried to dye it red once, but the color washed out within two days. Grace learned to live with it and embrace it, just as she did everything else that was weird in her life.

Charles' grin changed to a full blown smile. "Beautiful hair. I see it runs in the family," he said as he noted the same hair on all three women. Except for the amount of gray on her grandmothers and mothers, the thickness and length was exactly the same.

"That's not the only thing that runs in our family," Grace said with slight sarcasm.

Granny and mom gave out a grunt at her remark. Grace ignored it.

"How can I help you, Charles?"

"Richmond. My last name is Richmond," he said. "Is there any place we can talk privately?" he asked.

"You can go up to her apartment," Mom suggested.

Grace shot her an icy stare. Her place was a mess, and was in no mood to straighten up just to talk to someone.

Besides, if anything were to get personal, Grace wouldn't want it to start off with him thinking she was a slob.

"That would be great!" he said. "You lead the way."

Grace gritted her teeth as she led Charles up the back stairs to her apartment.

"I don't normally do private readings in my apartment," Grace said as she led him through the kitchen to living room.

"Oh, I'm not here for a reading."

"Then what are you here for?"

Grace motioned for him to take a seat while she cleared the coffee table of wrappers and empty beer cans.

"Let me give you a hand with that." Charles offered.

They dumped the trash into the recycling bins that Grace had stacked in the corner of her kitchen. She motioned for Charles to have a seat while she retrieved a brush from her bathroom. Grace sat across from him, brushing her hair, waiting to hear why he wanted to see her.

He watched intently as Grace ran the brush through her thick black hair. "You have amazing features."

Grace stopped in mid brush. "Thanks, but I don't think you came up here to talk about my hair."

"I'm not just talking about your hair. Your skin is like alabaster and your eyes are like ice green."

Grace felt her face flush at his compliment. She wasn't used to getting such exquisite compliments from anyone, let alone someone as good looking as Charles Richmond.

"It's an unusual trait of my Hungarian heritage."

"Is fortune telling a part of your Hungarian heritage as well?"

Grace nodded. "I'm the last in a long line of Hungarian gypsies." Grace gave Charles a brief history of her family roots, starting with her great grandmother.

He seemed quite interested in all that she had to say.

"We've talked enough about my family. You never told me why you're here." Grace reminded him.

"Forgive me." He apologized. "I'm here on police business."

He pulled out his badge and showed it to Grace.

Grace examined the badge and nodded at the authenticity.

"Have you heard of the murders that have been happening over the past few months?"

"I hear they found another body," Grace said.

He placed his badge back in his pocket. "Yesterday another woman was found in the same way as the other two. I won't know the details of her death until after the long weekend."

"I gather you think they're all connected?"

"So far, all the murders are linked and we believe that this one is another victim of the same person."

"And you are here, why?" Grace asked.

"We're at a dead end. We have no suspects."

"I don't know how I can help you."

Charles looked at Grace, and their eyes met. His eyes were large and soulful and she felt that same fuzzy feeling from earlier. She clenched her thighs tight to stop them from quivering.

There was something about this man that made her tingle, but wasn't sure if she wanted to know. Grace also tried to ignore the bright orange and yellow aura that surrounded him.

"You think we have a serial killer at work here?" Grace asked.

"I'm not supposed to say anything, but between us, yes. I do believe we've got a serial killer in Niagara Falls."

"What can I possibly do?"

"I know this sounds crazy, but when I was on the Toronto police force, there were a couple of officers who believed in this psychic stuff."

"But you weren't one of them?"

He shrugged his shoulders. "I've never had much of an opinion on it except that there must be some truth to it."

Grace tied her hair back in a pony tail. "I gather you're grasping at straws then in order for you to be here."

"Is there anything you can do to help us?"

"What are you looking for?" she asked.

"Apart from the killers' name, anything you can give me. I don't want to have another murder on our hands. But if this guy has killed three women in a short period of time, then he's ready to strike again soon."

"And you want to get him before he does," Grace finished his sentence.

"Yes."

There's more to this than he's telling me, Grace thought. "The last victim, was she from the area?"

"We think it's a possibility because the others were too. But we've no I.D. as of yet."

Niagara Falls was coming into the tourist season, and Grace couldn't help but think that his being here was more politically motivated than public safety.

"I know what you're thinking, and it couldn't be further from the truth," Charles said.

"Oh come on. You're telling me that the mayor hasn't been in touch with your captain about this?"

Graces' family had a history of problems when it came to the mayor and his council. Gang is more befitting to them. When Helga opened up shop back in the late forties, they tried to run her out of town.

From what Grace was told, you would think that it was something out of a Frankenstein movie where the villagers would show up with torches and pitch forks to drive the creature out of his domain.

Fortunately for Helga, the mayor's wife was a frequent guest to their home. She put the pressure on her husband to back off. Unfortunately for Helga, when a new mayor came into power, the scene would be played out again and again.

But there was always someone watching over them and they survived years of harassment to come to the point where they were allowed to open up a table on the main drag to entice tourists.

Charles became defensive. "What goes on between the captain and the mayor is no business of mine. I just want to catch this killer before he strikes again."

"Before his next victim is tourist and the word is leaked out about the problem the city has," Grace added.

Charles stood. "Look, if you don't want to help me, then I don't want to waste anymore of your time and mine."

"I didn't say I wouldn't help you. You need to tell me what it is you want me to do." Grace motioned Charles to sit.

Charles got a grip of his emotions. "I know that the people who run the tourist area of Lundy's Lane and the Hill are pretty close knit. They don't like outsiders butting in their business."

"That's putting it mildly," Grace replied.

"For starters, is there any way you can convince some of the locals to open up to me?" Charles asked.

Grace nodded. "I can try my best but I can't make any promises."

"Is there anything else?"

Charles' cheeks slightly reddened at his next request. "Is there any way you can use your talents to help us track this person?"

"Can you can bring me something that belonged to the victims?" Grace asked without skipping a beat.

"I can do that. When do you want them?"

"This afternoon would be good. I'll try and get something off of the items," she said.

Charles gave Grace a nod, and she walked him to the door.

"I'm curious about something," Grace asked as she opened the door.

"What's that?"

"How did you hear about us? It's obvious you're not from around here and it's not as if we're that well known outside the city."

He smiled, forming his perfect dimples on his perfect cheeks. They gave him a more boyish appearance than manly. "My partner knows you. Sarah Child."

Grace watched him hurry down the steps to his car as the rain pelted his body with cold drops. Grace stood there with mouth open and a shocked look on her face. She wasn't sure whether to call him back and say forget it or give Sarah Child a call and ask her who the hell she thinks she is.

It was too late to do anything. I made a commitment and I always keep my word, she thought, as she watched him start his car and pull out of the back lot.

FOUR

"I'm surprised you remember me," Becky said with excitement. "I guess the rain has put a damper on business."

"A little, so I thought I'd take this opportunity to take you out for a drive," Joe said.

"I'm glad you called me. I've never been to the city before. It's nice to have someone who lives in the area to take me around."

Joe smiled. "After seeing you at the bar I knew I had to get to know you."

Becky smiled back. "I'm glad you did. Meeting you has made this trip with my parent more bearable."

Joe glanced over at his companion. "So where did you say you were from?"

Becky leaned back in her seat. She was young and pretty. Her body was petite, her hair naturally red. "New Hampshire. Ever been?"

Joe shook his head. "I don't get to travel much with my business."

Becky bit her bottom lip. "Well, maybe you can come visit me sometime," she suggested.

"Maybe," he replied.

"So why did you come here with your parents?" Joe asked, changing the subject.

She rolled her brown eyes and sighed deeply. "My parents decided to drag me here against my will."

"I hope they don't mind me taking you out."

"They don't know I'm out with you." Becky giggled. "I told them I was going to do a little souvenir shopping for my friends."

"That's cool," Joe responded.

Becky crossed her arms and gave out a huff. "They treat me like a child. I mean, I'm eighteen after all. Why can't they just treat me like an adult?"

Joe sat silent as he turned down a dirt road. The rain was getting heavier as they approached the old farm house.

Becky looked around and began to feel uncomfortable. "Where are we?" she asked nervously.

Joe reached over and touched her hand. "I live here," he said, trying to reassure her.

Becky strained to see the house through the rain soaked window. "Why are we here?"

"I'm sorry. I thought the rain would let up a bit but seeing that it hasn't, I thought I'd grab some raincoats and umbrellas so we can walk around in a few of the parks I want to show you," he said as he cut the engine of his pickup truck. "We'll only be a minute."

Becky noticed the upstairs windows were boarded up, and an uneasy feeling came over her.

Becky didn't move. "I can wait here," she suggested. "You aren't afraid, are you? Cause if you are, I can take you back to your parents."

Becky swallowed hard. "Of course not. I just don't want to get wet."

Joe gave out a laugh. "Come on. I have towels if you get wet. Besides, I want to show you my collection of exotic fish."

She still didn't budge.

Frustration began to build inside Joe. "Okay, fine. I'll take you back to the falls and drop you off at your hotel." He started the engine.

Becky bit her lip again. She didn't want to spend the day cooped up with her parents in a hotel room. "Okay, as long as we only stay for a few minutes."

Grace pulled her coat over her head as she headed down the stairs to her car. It was close to eleven and the Summers twins needed a ride to work.

The Summers family consisted of ten children ranging in age from thirty-two to three years old. All were boys and all had ginger skin with unmanageable orange hair.

Ricky and Robby Summers had turned eighteen and just like their older brothers, they graduated to working in the family business every weekend as well as through the summer. The family business was the haunted mansion on Lundy's Lane.

When Grace was twelve, Ralph Summers decided to step up the business by having real people do the scaring. The mechanical creatures would always break down and they didn't have the scare that he wanted for his haunted house.

He closed the haunted mansion for the winter and spent a ton of money on renovations. Most of which consisted of black curtains for the hired help to hide behind.

When spring rolled along the following year, he had a private opening for all the local shop owners.

Grace and her family were among the first to walk through the new haunted mansion.

Although Ralph had a head for business, the man didn't know the difference between a hammer and a nail. In theory his plan was genius. Where else could you walk through a haunted mansion and have real people jump at you or grab you by the ankle?

In theory it would have worked too if it weren't for Grace's grandmother finding a flaw in the exhibit. That flaw happened while her family walked through the haunted mansion.

Ralph wanted to scare the hell out of granny and waited in the darkest part of the exhibit for her. As Grace and her mother passed by him he jumped out from behind a curtain and scared the bejeezus out of granny.

She shrieked and her right foot made contact with his baby maker and two bowling buddies. Ralph grabbed his jewels and hit the floor with a thud. Grace lost her shoe as they ran screaming from the haunted mansion, leaving Grace's shoe and poor Ralph Summers behind, lying in a fetal position.

The next day Ralph's wife, Angela, closed the mansion for more renovations. She had some workers erect walls that moved along a track. This allowed the hired ghouls to move the walls and hide as they waited for customers to pass by. This also gave them protection from frightened customers whose reflexes were similar in nature to Grace's grandmother.

Ralph Summers healed from his attack and went on to have five more children. Unfortunately Grace's shoe was never found along with the odd shoe left behind by other customers.

For many years Grace believed the mansion was located on top of a vortex and when all the renovations began, Summers opened a small part of that vortex that only a single shoe could go through. That was until she saw their lost and found in the lobby. The box was full of shoes. All single shoes. Hers was never among them.

The haunted mansion became a success and still operated in the same fashion except for a few changes. There were ghouls who lay in bathtubs dripping with fake blood.

When people would approach, the ghoul would raise his or her head and bang chains against the tub. Others would walk behind a group of people and when someone would turn around they would try to grab them before they ran off.

Grace thought about going through to see the new exhibits but never did. Partly since her first time scarred her for life and secondly because of the oldest boy, Jeremy.

Jeremy and Grace went through school together. He was one of the few friends she had growing up since he was a bit of a freak himself. His ginger looks and wild orange hair made it impossible for him to blend in a crowd.

Rumors were spread through high school that she lost her virginity to him. Unfortunately the rumors were somewhat true. Although they never really went all the way, he did manage to get a feel of her boobs.

How the rumor got started was easy to figure out. He became pretty popular after that and she received the new title of slut. Grace didn't mind that title so much. It got her lots of dates none of which got to feel her boobies.

Her friendship with Jeremy was strained since that day.

Grace pulled into the Summers driveway and honked the horn. The Summers twin came bouncing down the steps, their hair flying wildly in the rain. They climbed into the back seat, and waved to the mother.

"How's it going?" they asked as Grace backed out of the driveway.

"It goes good. How goes it with you two?" she replied.

"Excellent! We're working at the mansion. What a cool job," Ricky said.

"Yeah. We get to scare the shit out of these old farts. I just hope one of them doesn't end up have a coronary right there in front of us." Robby added.

"Doesn't your father have that sign posted at the entrance that if you have a heart condition you shouldn't enter?"

"Yeah but no one ever reads it anyway," Ricky said.

"By the way, Jeremy says hey," Robby said.

"How's he doing?"

"Doing good. He and Melanie are expecting their second kid in December," Robby said. "The first one came out with blonde hair like Melanie's. Maybe this'll be the end of this freakin hair of ours."

"I don't know. Your hair's not that bad," Grace said, glancing in the rearview mirror.

Ricky grunted. "You try having people take you serious when you look like a freak."

"You work in a haunted mansion scaring people. How can you expect anyone to take you serious when you're doing that?"

Ricky thought for a moment. "Good point."

Grace smiled at the twins as she pulled into the back lot of the mansion.

"There you go boys," she said as she pulled up to the employee's entrance. "Safe and sound."

"Thanks for the ride," they said. "Why don't you come in for a free tour?"

Grace shook her head. "Thanks but no thanks. I can't afford to lose another shoe."

They laughed. "Oh yeah. We forgot about that one."

"I guess it would be nuts of me to ask if you ever found it."

"Yep that would be nuts." Robby laughed.

"Why don't you come in sometime and be one of the actors? It's so cool to dress up in costume and go around scaring people," Robby asked.

Grace laughed. "That would be fun. I might just do that sometime."

They waved to Grace then ducked their lanky bodies in the employee's door. Grace did a U-turn and made a left on Lundy's Lane and headed back home.

Although the rain hadn't let up, this didn't stop some adventurous tourists from taking in the sights.

I wish I could erect an enclosure for my readings, Grace thought as she drove the distance home.

An umbrella, table and two chairs aren't cutting it when it comes to the rain. A small booth or enclosure would let me work on days like today. Grace sighed.

Grace pulled in the parking lot then walked around the corner to the adult store next door.

Sue was rearranging merchandise as Grace walked in the door.

"Hey, Sue," Grace yelled as she shook the water off her coat and hung it up behind the counter. "The rain put a damper on my business today."

Sue greeted Grace with the usual toothy smile outlined in black lipstick. "Same here, so I thought I'd try to straighten up a bit."

"Need some help?" Grace offered.

"For sure. Can you put the videos back in their right place for me?" Sue asked pointing a stack of videos on the counter.

Sue's mother owned a chain of adult specialty stores that carried anything from adult videos for sale and rent to vibrators of all shapes and sizes, to role playing outfits. She was only a couple of years behind Grace in school, but Grace never could remember her growing up.

Her family lived in the area for generations. She even had some native Indian somewhere along her bloodline, but not enough to allow her the privileges that came along with being a native.

When she was in high school, she developed a love for everything gothic, and never lost her passion for it. She still wore her black nail polish and white paste makeup and had an array of piercings on her face and parts unknown. Her hair was dyed black, but she could never get it as black as Graces' hair without it turning blue.

Today she added streaks of fuchsia that framed her face. Somehow her appearance suited her surroundings of adult paraphernalia. No one ever seemed to blink an eye at her appearance when they entered the store. But then again, they were, after all, browsing an adult sex store.

"I see you changed your hair," Grace said as she looked over the adult videos and placed them where she thought they might belong.

"Yeah. Thought I'd add some feminine touch to my look. What do you think?"

Grace and Sue developed a close friendship in the five years Sue worked in her mother's store, and Grace had yet to see her in anything feminine.

Unless you call fishnet stockings, black combat boots, and a leather skirt that was an inch below her hoohah, feminine.

Grace examined her appearance more closely. "It matches the black and fuchsia striped tights you're wearing, and it doesn't make your face look so much like death warmed over."

Sue gave out a laugh. "Damn! I was hoping that wouldn't be the case. I guess I need to work on that death look a little more."

Grace grinned. "Anything new in the wig department?"

Sue snapped her fingers and ducked into the back room. "As a matter of fact, we had a shipment a couple days ago on wigs. I just haven't had a chance to put them out."

Grace followed her into the back room and inspected the new wigs.

"Have a seat," Sue said, pushing Grace into a nearby chair.

She started by pinning up Graces' thick hair in order to fit a tight net over her head so she could try on all the wigs. "You need to thin this hair of yours out." She grunted as she used pin after pin.

"I already did that. It just made it thicker."

After which seemed like a zillion pins, Sue stepped back to look at her handiwork. "Well, I managed to get it all up, but maybe if you layered it, it would be easier to manage."

Grace did a mental eye roll. This advice about her hair was coming from a girl whose idea of changing her hair was to add florescent colors to it.

"Maybe I will next haircut."

They both held their breath as Sue pulled the snug stocking over Graces' pinned up hair. She then pulled out a long platinum wig with loose curls and fitted it on top of her head. She stood back to examine the placement.

Grace smiled widely as she saw how beautiful the wig looked on her. "I wish I could get my hair this color."

"It looks great on you. Why don't you keep it?" Sue smiled.

Grace thought about it for a moment and decided against it.

"It would give my family a heart attack if they saw me with this wig."

"They don't have to know. Just wear it when you want to go out."

Grace shrugged. "Maybe I could do that. Okay I'll take it."

Grace looked at the price tag and gave out a gulp. "A little too rich for my blood."

"It's a gift," Sue said. "Think of it as an early birthday present."

"Your mother will kill you."

Sue waved her hand. "I ordered it for you myself. She doesn't even know."

The door buzzed as a customer interrupted their conversation.

"Be right back," Sue said. "And don't take it off!" she ordered as she disappeared to the front of the store.

"I'm looking for Grace," a familiar voice said. "Would she happen to be here?"

"That would all depend on why you're looking for her." Sue responded.

Grace walked out to the front of the store, still wearing the blonde wig.

Charles was standing at the counter and took a double take at Grace in the blonde wig. "Wow!" His eyes widened, and he grinned ear to ear.

"You know this guy?" Sue asked.

Grace gave a nod. "Yes, he came to my place earlier. He's a detective investigating those murders that have been happening in the area."

Sue's blinked twice. "You're a cop?"

Charles smiled. "Yes, I am."

"You don't look like a cop."

"Is that so? Then what do I look like to you?"

Grace tried to intercede. "You really don't want Sue to answer that, do you?"

Grace loved Sue but even she knew that loaded questions got loaded answers from her friend.

Charles' laughed. "I guess that would depend on whether her answer is a compliment or not."

"Oh, it definitely would be," Sue purred.

Grace rolled her eyes. "How can I help you, officer?" she asked, changing the subject.

"If this isn't a bad time, I thought we could get a head start on what we discussed earlier. I brought in some of the items that you requested."

"Not a bad time at all," Grace assured him. "We can go up to my apartment so I can look over what you have."

Love and Murder on the Hill

Grace gave Sue a wave and she gave her *a thumbs up*. "I'll see you later," Grace said.

Charles held the door open for Grace. "I thought you had dark hair?" he asked as she walked past him.

"Holy crap! I forgot about the wig." Grace put her hands on her head and went back into the store. "Be right back," she said, handing him the keys to her apartment. "Let yourself in, and I'll be with you shortly."

Ten minutes later they were sitting in her living room, looking through the folders and items that Charles brought.

"Not to go off topic, but you looked great in the blonde wig." He smiled.

Graces' cheeks flushed, and she felt that familiar fuzzy feeling from earlier that day. "You think so?" she asked, fishing for another compliment.

"Most definitely. But if I had to choose between blonde and your natural black hair, I'd choose the black."

Grace ran her fingers through her hair. "You like this better? I thought all men loved blondes."

"Don't get me wrong. I love blondes, too. As a matter of fact, I love all hair colors. But with the blonde, you look like everyone else. With the black hair, you stand out in the crowd."

"Just what I needed, to stand out in the crowd," she moaned.

"What's wrong with being different?"

"Don't get me wrong. I like the idea of being different, too. But all my life I've been different from everyone else. And I don't mean that in a positive way." A slight sense of sadness overtook Grace as she recalled her childhood. She tried to shake the feeling off by concentrating on the folders in front of her.

Charles' eyes never left Grace. He could sense her mood change. "It must have been rough growing up in your family of fortune tellers." His voice softened and felt soothing.

Grace shrugged. "It wasn't easy. But when I look back at how great my mother and grandmother were to me, I wouldn't change it for the world."

Grace's face lit up and her mood changed to a more positive one. "Besides, all the people who run the shops and tourist shows on the Hill are my friends. Some of them I've known forever."

"That must have been fun for you," Charles said.

Grace nodded. "At the very least it was interesting."

Charles moved closer and touched her hand. He leaned in and kissed Grace on the lips, catching her off guard.

Grace felt a warm sensation start at her lips and end at her southern 'V' zone.

"What was that for?" she asked as she moved away slightly.

His face blushed, and he suddenly became awkward. "I'm sorry. I shouldn't have done that. I just felt you needed a kiss. I hope I didn't offend you."

Grace put her fingers to her lips. His kiss left her body quivering. He didn't offend Grace. If anything, he gave her goose bumps and she had this overwhelming urge to jump his bones right then. Grace resisted.

"No. You didn't offend me. You just caught me off guard."

Grace fumbled over her words. Best to keep my mouth shut, she thought, before she says something that might encourage another kiss.

Not that Grace wouldn't have welcomed it. But two kisses would mean ending up sweaty and naked on the floor. The fact that they just met, Grace wasn't about to give herself that easily, no matter how desperate and horny she was.

"Maybe we should work on this case before anything else happens," Grace suggested.

Charles gave her a sideways glance. "Like what?"

FIVE

Joe unlocked the door to his house and held it open for Becky. "Hurry before we get drenched," he said as he ushered her inside the dark room.

Rain pelted the windows as Joe flipped on a light, exposing the meager furnished room. Clothes lay scattered around the room as if it had been ransacked.

"Sorry about the mess," he apologized as he quickly gathered the laundry to make room for Becky.

Becky smiled, and her uneasiness left her as she watched Joe race around gathering his belongings.

She helped by gathering a few dirty dishes. "Where should I put these?" she asked, holding some cups and plates she meticulously stacked together.

Joe piled the clothes in an empty laundry basket and took the dirty dishes from Becky. "As you can tell by the mess, I don't normally get visitors." He again apologized as he stacked the dishes in the sink.

"That's okay." Becky said. "I'm sure it's an organized mess."

"Why don't you have a seat, while I fix us something to drink."

Becky's smile disappeared, and her uneasiness returned.

"Isn't it a little early to be drinking? Besides, I thought we were just grabbing some raincoats?"

Joe glanced over at his guest, and sensed her hesitation. "It's my famous cappuccino. I promise once you taste it, you won't find one better."

Becky began to relax, and her smile returned. "I could use a good cappuccino."

Joe pointed his right index finger at his guest. "You got it! Make yourself at home while I create the best cappuccino ever."

Charles laid out four clear baggies on the coffee table. Each one had a different item.

Grace picked up the first baggie and examined the watch. "Is it okay to remove the items from the bags?" she asked.

Charles nodded and Grace unzipped the bag and removed the watch.

She fondled the watch between her fingers, rubbing her hands up and down the worn leather straps.

"I'm going to concentrate on each item and I need you to be very quiet." Grace instructed. "I'll record everything that I say in regards to each item."

She flipped on her tape recorder then closed her eyes, all the while feeling the watch between her fingers.

"This belonged to the most recent victim. Dark hair, dark eyes," Grace said.

She moved the watch close to her cheek and stroked her face with it. "She knows her killer. She's pleased that he asked her out on a date."

Grace stopped for a moment and became uneasy. "He offered her a drink. It tastes good but has made her dizzy." Grace put the watch down and opened her eyes.

Charles sat in silence as Grace put the watch back in the bag and picked up another bag that contained a white tee shirt. There's dried blood stains on the front of the shirt and this sent chills through Grace.

She rubbed the collar of the shirt between her forefinger and thumb. Her eyes closed and her expression was distorted. "This victim was his third victim and she suffered more than the first," She said. "Oh such violence. She tried to escape and she fought him. She can't understand why he is doing this to her. She thought he liked her."

Grace touched her head. "He hit her with something. She's still alive but unconscious."

Grace opened her eyes and tears fell down her cheeks. She put the shirt back in its bag and wiped away her tears.

"Are you okay?" Charles asked.

Grace nodded without saying a word and picked up the next item. This time a small birthstone ring was removed from the bag. As with the first two items, Grace touched the ring and closed her eyes.

She put it on her left pinkie. "The second victim wears her ring on this finger. Her killer told her how nice the ring was. He wanted to keep the ring as a souvenir but couldn't get it off her finger."

Love and Murder on the Hill

Grace took a deep breath as she touched the ring with her other hand. "It smells musty here. She's strapped to a table and it's cold and damp. She can't see anything. It's too dark." Grace became uneasy and opened her eyes. She put the ring back in the baggie and picked up the last bag.

Grace looked at the necklace and removed it from the bag. She repeated her display and closed her eyes. "This one is different," she said. "He knows her more than the others. They were lovers."

Grace wrapped the chain around her fingers. "She was his first victim but her death was an accident."

"She's covered with something. Hidden from view."

"If you find her, you'll find her killer," Grace said.

She opened her eyes and placed the necklace back in the bag.

Charles' eyes widened. "What do you mean find her?"

"Just what I said. You need to find her to find the killer."

Charles shook his head in disbelief. "You mean to say there's another victim out there and we haven't found her body yet?"

Grace stood and walked to the kitchen, opened the refrigerator and poured two glasses of orange juice. She returned to the living room and handed a glass to Charles.

"Thanks," he said taking the glass from her.

Grace sat next to Charles, and sipped her juice. "Let me ask you something," she said between sips. Where did you find the necklace?"

"We found it at the same time as the last body. It was up river from the body in the mud along the river bank," he said.

"The area was searched well?" she asked.

Charles nodded. It was pretty open and we combed as far down the shore as we could," he said. "Where I found the necklace, was farther up the shore. I couldn't go any farther without falling in.

Grace thought for a moment. "I don't think the body is in Niagara Falls. He put her somewhere else," Grace said. Where all the bodies were found is not where he put them."

Where would he be dumping the bodies to have them end up where they've ended up?" Charles asked.

"He's dumping them above the falls," Grace replied.

"That doesn't make sense. The only way that a body can travel over the falls is if it were dropped in the tourist area at the bottom of Clifton Hill," Charles said.

"And that would be impossible without being seen," Grace added."

Charles nodded. "If he disposed of the bodies farther up river, there is an almost zero chance they'd make it over the falls without being seen."

"Or even make it that far," Graced said.

Charles sighed and rubbed his forehead as he felt a headache coming on. "I think we have another mystery on our hands."

"We have more than that," Grace said.

"What are you talking about?"

Grace sighed deeply. "He has another girl."

The color drained from Charles' face as he rubbed his hands over his eyes. "This is exactly what I was afraid of."

"I'm so sorry Charles," Grace said.

Charles stared into Graces' eyes. "Are you sure he has someone else? Maybe you're mistaken."

Grace shook her head. "There's no mistake. Henry told me during my trance."

"Henry?" Charles looked puzzled.

"My spirit guide," she said.

"Now I'm really confused." Charles leaned back on the sofa and took a big gulp of his orange juice. It got stuck for a moment then edged its way down his throat.

"Maybe I should explain this to you," she said.

"You see, some real psychics have a main spirit they communicated with from another dimension. This spirit or guide talks to them about what they're searching for," Grace said.

Grace continued to explain how she is given the information she's searching for.

"Some spirits even have a name and a past life. My spirit was a man named Henry who'd been a slave. He died trying to escape his owners and was eventually captured and killed. He's been communicating beyond the grave with me since my abilities became known."

"Does he talk to you all the time?" Charles asked.

"Always when I'm in a trance, like today," Grace replied. But sometimes he'll come to me while I'm sleeping and that drives me crazy because he won't shut up. Sometimes he would go on about his life in the South before the war."

Grace finished her juice and took the empty glasses to the kitchen. Charles followed and took a place at the small, dated kitchen table.

"He's a tortured soul and finds comfort with me."

Love and Murder on the Hill

"Why doesn't he move on?" Charles asked.

Grace shrugged. "I've asked myself the same question. I've tried to help him but he won't leave. Henry has a lot of anger and hate. He needs to let go of that in order to pass on and be reborn. Unfortunately, Henry isn't the type of spirit who takes advice easily."

"So you're stuck with a guy who was a slave who has anger issues," Charles said.

"That's about the size of it." Grace replied. "My mother told me when my soul passes on, only then will Henry pass on too."

"This is so fascinating," Charles said. "I never knew there's so much involved with fortune telling."

"Not as fascinating as one would think. Sometimes when Henry is in one of his moods, I find it hard to sleep." Grace took a deep breath and joined Charles at the table.

"Anyway, whatever his reasons for refusing to let go are his alone. And because of this we're joined together in a psychic marriage," she added.

They sat in silence while Charles absorbed all the information Grace gave him. He'd never experienced anything like he'd just witnessed and all this talk about spirits being married to living beings was making his head hurt.

Grace removed the tape from the recorder and slipped it in its case. "You don't look so good," she said as she handed Charles the tape.

"Do you have any aspirin?" he asked taking the tape from her. "I feel a headache coming on."

"I have just the thing," she said.

Grace took a box of loose tea and some cheese cloth from the cupboard.

She filled the cheese cloth with some of the tea, tied it in a knot, and popped it in a mug. She filled the mug with water and stuck it in the microwave on high for sixty seconds.

"This'll sooth your head without conventional synthetic medicines."

The microwave beeped and Grace removed to mug. She took out the bag and added a drop of honey to the steaming tea. "Sip on this. It'll make you feel better," she said, handing him the mug.

They returned to the living room where Charles sipped his hot tea. "This tastes pretty good," he said.

"Thanks," Grace replied. "It's a family recipe.

"I'm curious about something," Charles said. "How does this guy manage to get these women to trust him?"

"He lures them with his good looks and charm. He's the kind of guy who women want to date," Grace said. "A real smooth talker."

"How does he overpower them?" Charles asked.

"He drugs them. He makes them a drink, and he puts something in it."

"Based on what you said, it sounds like this guy is a local."

Grace nodded. "He has to be to get the bodies to end up where they are."

"The problem with him being local is that it's difficult to get anyone on the Hill to talk to the police."

Grace understood exactly where Charles was coming from.

The people on the Hill were a close knit family. They watched each other's backs and if the police were snooping around asking questions about one of them, they wouldn't get anywhere. No one ever ratted out one of their kind to the cops, even if one of their kind was running around killing people.

"I could try and find out if anyone knows anything," Grace suggested.

"You'd do that?"

She nodded. "If one of our people is out there picking up young girls and raping and killing them, I'd want them stopped just as much as you would."

Charles smiled at Grace as he sipped on his tea.

They sat in silence listening to the rain hit the window.

"You know, you've got an incredible talent," he said.

Grace felt her cheeks blush.

"I'm serious. You have a special gift. I was completely hypnotized by what you were doing. You said things that only someone who was close to the case would have known."

"I get the feeling that you coming here with a last ditch effort for help, yet you weren't completely convinced of my abilities," Grace said.

"Not at all. I believe there's some truth to everything," he said. "But you have to admit there's a lot of fakes out there."

"There are many fakes in every field. My profession happens to get a bad rap because the fakes prey on the desperate."

Love and Murder on the Hill

"But I'm not a fake. I'm the real deal. Just like my mother and my grandmother," Grace said.

Charles could sense dissatisfaction in her voice. "I'm sorry if I said the wrong thing or made you feel as if I was skeptical. I wouldn't be here if I truly felt you were a fake."

Grace patted Charles' knee. "That's okay officer. I'm used to the skeptics."

"Well shucks maam. Thanks for understanding," Charles said in his best John Wayne impersonation.

"I hope that I can help you with this case." Grace said with a slight southern drawl.

They both laughed and leaned back on the large overstuffed sofa.

Charles finished his tea and put his cup on the coffee table.
"Headache gone?" Grace asked.
"Yep. Sure is."
"What do you want to do now?" Grace asked.
"I don't know. Got anything in mind?"
"Have you ever had your tarot cards read?"
"Can't say that I have."

Grace hauled herself off the sofa, moved to the bedroom and returned a moment later with her worn cards.

They moved to the kitchen and Grace handed Charles the cards. She sat across from him and instructed him to shuffle the cards then cut them into three piles while making a wish.

He sat silently absorbing what Grace told him of his past, present, and future. She told him how his family wasn't disappointed with his choice to pursue a career as a police officer. She told him his family only wishes he would settle down with someone.

"Will I meet that someone?" he asked just above a whisper.

Grace looked up at him, and their gaze met. She looked down at the cards and studied them. "You already have. But you don't know it yet. Neither does this special person."

"Will I get my wish?" he asked gently as if he were afraid of being overheard.

Grace studied the cards again. "Most definitely," she said with a smile.

He took a deep breath and exhaled. "Do you have any plans for supper?"

Grace gathered the cards and stacked them together. "Do you want to make any?"

He nodded. "Why don't you let me take you out to a nice restaurant for a wonderful meal, and we can get to know each other on a more personal level without the use of tarot cards?"

"Sounds good to me." Grace grinned ear to ear.

Joe handed Becky a cup of hot cappuccino. "Tell me what you think of the coffee," he said as he sat beside her.

She took a sip and wiped the froth from her lips. "Yum. You're right. This is the best cappuccino I've ever tasted."

Joe gave Becky and approving smile. "I'm glad you like it."

Joe watched Becky as she finished her drink. "Would you like another?" he asked, taking the cup from her.

"That would be nice," she replied.

"Just relax, and I'll get you another hot one."

He disappeared into the kitchen, returning a minute later, and handed Becky a fresh cup of Italian coffee. She took a sip and gave out a yawn.

"Are you okay?" Joe asked. "You look sleepy."

Becky put the cup down and covered her mouth as she yawned again. "I don't know. I just feel a bit tired."

"Could be the weather," Joe suggested. "Sometimes the rain will make a person sleepy."

Becky felt herself become light-headed. She tried to focus on her surroundings, but the room began to spin out of control.

She suddenly became painfully aware Joe had drugged her.

"I want to go home," she cried.

Joe stood and took the cup from Becky. He extended his hand and slapped Becky in the face. "You ain't going nowhere, bitch!" he snarled.

Becky fell to the floor and slowly tried to stand. The room became blurry and there was a buzzing sound in her ears.Joe placed his foot on Becky's back, pushing her back down to the floor.

The sound of his voice faded in and out as the buzzing became louder.

She felt his hands tug on her, pulling her across the floor as blackness engulfed her and everything went silent.

SIX

"Where you off to?" Mom asked as she and granny sat in Grace's living room.

Grace was busy figuring out what to wear and finally settled on a little black dress with tiny straps. One could never go wrong with a black dress.

"I have a date tonight," Grace replied.

Granny and mom looked at each other and grinned. "I don't suppose it's with that handsome detective?" Mom asked.

Grace turned and looked in their direction. She narrowed her eyes at them as she felt the hairs on the back of her neck stand to attention.

"What's with the smiles?" Grace asked suspiciously.

"Oh, nothing," they said in unison. "We're just happy to see you go out for a change."

Grace could tell by the look on their faces that it was more than just being happy she was going out, but she felt it better to not dig any deeper.

A knock on the door saved Grace from further conversation.

"Mom, can you answer the door? I'm not quite ready," Grace asked as she ducked back into her bedroom and closed the door.

There was a three-way conversation going on when Grace finally emerged from the bedroom. "So what are the three of you talking about?" she asked as she joined her date and family in the living room.

Charles stood as Grace entered the room. His face brightened when he saw her. "You look beautiful," he said. His eyes scanned Grace from head to toe.

"No blonde wig," she laughed as she pointed to her head.

Catherine Angelone

He nodded in agreement. Mom and granny looked puzzled.

"Blonde wig? Don't tell me you've been going next door trying on wigs again," Granny said.

Grace gave them a sly grin. "I think we should be going," Grace said as she took her coat from the closet.

Charles helped Grace on with her coat, and they said good-bye to her family.

He held the car door for Grace, and she slid into the passenger seat. She watched him as he walked around to the driver's side and slid in beside her.

He he started the car, and they drove out of the parking lot, heading down Lundy's Lane toward Stanley Avenue.

"So what did you and my family talk about while I was getting ready?" Grace asked, breaking the silence in the car.

"Your family is quite interesting."

Grace looked sideways at him. "Interesting as in they should be locked up in the nut house or interesting as in they're fun to be with?"

Charles gave out a laugh. "Fun to be with, of course."

Ten minutes later they were seated in Casa Vecchia restaurant enjoying a glass of wine.

The decor was the stereo type Italian restaurant, with red checkered table cloths that were lit with tapered candles stuck in old wine bottles. The walls were covered with white stucco that saw better days and dark paneled wainscoting that was as authentic and weathered as the rest of the décor.

Their table was situated in a cozy corner of the restaurant, away from the other patrons and prying eyes. Grace was getting the feeling that this was prearranged.

Charles took the liberty to order pumpkin tortellini for the both of them.

"How did you know that I love tortellini?" she asked.

Charles just grinned.

"So that's what you and my family were talking about," Grace asked as a light went off in her brain.

"They told me that you loved Italian food and your favorite was pumpkin tortellini," he said as he sipped his wine.

Grace did a mental eye roll. "I can just imagine what else the three of you talked about." she sighed.

Love and Murder on the Hill

Charles moved closer. "Well, they told me that you haven't had a date in over two years. I guess they're worried since you spend a lot of time in the adult sex shop next door."

Grace felt another eye roll coming on. "Why am I not surprised by this?"

He leaned back in his chair and took another sip of wine. "They sure did. Can you imagine the look on my face when your grandmother suggested I stay the night with you?"

Grace put her hands over her ears. "I can't believe I'm hearing this."

Grace had been thinking of Charles since he left her place. She couldn't get him and his tight butt out of her head. Her mother and grandmother were right when they suggested he stay the night. She needed some hot steamy animal sex, and she couldn't think of any better partner than Charles.

Charles took her hands and kissed them gently. "Don't be embarrassed," he said. "I have no intention of taking advantage of you, unless, of course, you want me to."

Grace narrowed her eyes at him. She wasn't sure if he was joking or was dead serious.

"Do you think you could take advantage of me?" she asked.

Charles looked puzzled. "What do you mean?"

"What I mean is do you think you have it in you to get to third base with me?"

"Do you want me to go to third base with you or is this one of those games where there's some foreplay then bluffing involved?"

Grace batted her eyelashes. "Honey if I want you to go all the way with me I would just let you."

Charles grinned. "I sense a challenge coming on here."

"No challenge. I just think we should see what the evening brings us," she said.

Charles raised his glass. "To an exciting evening full of surprises."

Grace joined him in his toast. "Let's hope there aren't any boobie prizes at the end of the evening," she laughed.

"I hope there are at least two boobies at the end of this evening," Charles added.

The waiter arrived with their appetizers and a basket of rolls. Grace selected a warm roll and used her hands to break it apart.

"I bet you've led an interesting life with your family history," Charles said, changing the subject.

Grace dipped a piece of roll in the flavored oil and popped it in her mouth. "I wouldn't call it interesting actually."

Charles gave her a look of curiosity. "What would you call it but interesting? You grew up with women who have this incredible ability, or gift, as you call it, and you also inherited it. You had séances for party entertainment and sell crystals and good luck herbs as well as books on fortune telling."

"I suppose it's interesting if you minus the name calling, and the rock throwing, and not having any friends," she said.

"The people who did those things were stupid and blind. If they couldn't see how special you really are, then they don't deserve your friendship." His voice was warm and soothing.

"Would that include your partner, Sarah Child?" she asked.

Grace felt the old feelings coming back. She gave her body a preverbal shake to rid herself of the pain from her childhood.

"Sarah teased you when you both were young?" Charles asked.

Grace took a sip of wine. "Not at first. We became friends when she moved to the area," Grace said.

Their food arrived and Grace bit into a piece of tortellini. She closed her eyes and savored the morsel.

"This really is good," Charles said as he tasted his food.

"Yep. The best in town," Grace replied.

"So tell me more about you and Sarah."

Grace gave Charles a sideways glance. "You're not going to let this go are you?"

He shook his head. "No way. She's my partner and if she has a dark side, I need to know about it."

Grace moved her fork around her plate. "It's not really a dark side. We met around the age of eight. I invited her over for a sleep over and my grandmother and mother thought it would be fun to have a séance."

Charles tried to refrain himself from breaking out laughing. "You're joking right?"

Grace shook her head. "I wish I was. The poor thing laid awake all night in a fetal position waiting for dawn. I never saw anyone run screaming from my house before. As a matter of fact, I never saw anyone run screaming from anywhere. Well except maybe the haunted mansion on Lundy's Lane."

"What happened after that?" Charles asked.

"Her mother called my mother and gave her royal shit. She said how she was going to have to put poor Sarah in for therapy because of what happened."

"Did she go for therapy?"

Grace shrugged. "I don't know. We never spoke again. I haven't heard her name mentioned to me until you told me she was your partner."

Charles cleaned his plate free of tortellini. "Does it bother you that she's my partner?" he asked.

"A little, but this is just one date. It's not like we're getting married or anything like that," Grace said.

"The night's still young and we are in the honeymoon capital of the world." He smiled.

Grace rolled her eyes at Charles' remark.

"There's a bright side to all this," Charles said.

Grace narrowed her eyes. "Oh really? Do tell because I've been trying to find a bright side to my childhood all my life."

"The bright side is that at least the village idiots didn't try to storm your house with torches and pitch forks and try to run you out of town," he said.

Grace glanced over at him, and their eyes met. His smile and his words made her break out in full stomach laughter.

They both broke out in laughter.

"You've got a point there. They didn't try to torch our house and burn it to the ground," Grace added.

"Or tie you to a post and burn you and your family at the stake," he said between laughs.

They spent the remaining time cracking jokes and laughing at their silliness.

"Shall we order dessert, or are you one of those girls who never eat sweets?" he asked as they looked over the dessert menu.

"Are you kidding? Try and keep a cookie away from me. I could sniff one out in a ten mile radius."

"A woman after my own heart! What should we order?"

Grace looked over the menu but nothing caught her eye. "I don't know. Nothing seems to jump out at me."

He took the menu from her and laid them on the table. "I have a better idea."

Now I'm intrigued," Grace said.

He motioned for the waiter. "Check please."

Ten minutes later we were parked in front of Dairy Queen eating a large double dipped cone.

"How did you know that I love ice cream?" Grace asked.

"Everyone loves ice cream. Besides, if all else fails in life, eat ice-cream."

Grace took a lick of her cone. "That sounds like something my mother would say."

Charles gave Grace a sideways glance. "Okay I'm busted. Your mother did mention how much you love your ice cream."

Grace put her hand to her head as she felt brain freeze coming on. "Damn. They must have told you my life story while you were waiting for me."

Charles smiled. "Not much more than that. Except I did mention to them that I don't sleep with someone on the first date."

Grace gave out a cough and for a moment thought that ice cream was coming through her nose. "I really hope you're joking," she said between coughs.

Charles leaned back and laughed hardily. "Of course I'm joking. Do you honestly think I wouldn't sleep with someone on the first date?"

Grace punched Charles in the arm. "I wasn't talking about that."

"I'm joking about saying anything to your family," he said rubbing his arm. "Ow that hurt."

"Besides, it's not what you would say to them that would shock me. It's more what they would say to you."

They sat for a moment contemplating their next words. "So is that true? You'd sleep with someone on a first date if you had the opportunity?"

His smile widened. "Wanna find out?" He laughed.

"Maybe at the end of the date," she replied.

"Tell me about your childhood," she asked, changing the subject.

Charles moaned with boredom. "My life was the opposite of yours. I came from a life of privilege, and I had a ton of friends. Only a few I call friends today, of course."

"Of course," Grace said.

"My father was an entrepreneur who made his money in real estate. My mother was on every social committee from here to Ottawa," he continued.

"So they were stuffy upper-class?" she asked half jokingly.

"They were upper-class, but not as stuffy as some of the people they socialized with."

"How was it that you decided to go into law enforcement and not follow in your father's footsteps?"

He shrugged. "If I tell you, you promise not to repeat it?"

Grace held up her right hand. "I swear."

"When I was about eleven, me and a few friends from school decided to try our hand at graffiti. At least that's what I thought we were going to do."

Grace moved in closer as his voice lowered until he was speaking just above a whisper.

"Like an idiot, I showed up at our designated meeting area with five cans of spray paint."

"I gather the paint was never used?" Grace asked.

He shook his head. "The paint was used alright. They used it to paint pussy mobile on the side of our principal's car."

Grace burst out laughing and almost dropped her ice cream.

"It wasn't funny at the time," Charles said, trying not to laugh along. "These guys were a year or two older than me and I didn't find out till after the reason they wanted me along. I was to take the fall for them."

"They had you buy the paint so they could trace it back to you, and I bet the other boys had planned to be each other's alibi in case you talked," Grace said with a laugh.

"What did I know back then? I was a kid and thought these guys wanted to be my friend. They were so cool, and I just wanted to be like them."

"Boy that was dumb. I mean, you must have been the dumbest kid in school. I wasn't popular, but I wouldn't have been that desperate to do something so stupid just to fit in." Grace chuckled.

"Oh, thanks a lot," Charles said with hurt feelings.

Grace tried to regain her composure. "Oh please, I didn't mean it. I just think it's funny that someone who had everything would still have a need to be accepted."

Charles thought for a moment. "You're right about one thing."

"Oh? And what's that?"

Their eyes met, and Grace felt butterflies in her stomach. "It really was a stupid thing to do. And what made matters worse; I thought they were referring to cats. I thought our principal loved cats and that was why they wrote pussy."

Grace laughed so hard she almost peed her pants. "Do you still think he was into cats?"

"Anyway," he continued, ignoring her remark. "The principle called the police and, because of the situation they decided to give me community service." His voice turned serious. "Every weekend for three months I worked in a soup kitchen feeding the homeless."

His smile disappeared, and he lowered his head. "It broke my heart to see so many people with nothing. There were children who were so happy just to receive an extra helping of food."

Grace felt for him. If a person knew the exact moment when a person fell in love with someone, Grace would say it was at that very moment for her. She took his hand, leaned closer and kissed him on the forehead.

He sighed deeply as they sat silently eating the rest of their ice cream.

"Anyway, the good thing was that my parents helped these people by donating money to the soup kitchen and to the churches that used their basements for sleeping quarters. My mother arranged fundraisers with her society friends, and together they were able to raise a hundred thousand dollars the first year." His voice lost its sadness and was replaced with hopefulness.

"Was that when you decided to become a police officer?" Grace asked.

He shook his head. "I was about sixteen and every Sunday I would go to the soup kitchen to help out. This one particular Sunday I was wiping down tables when this little girl came up to me. Her hair looked as if it hadn't seen a brush or shampoo in a week. She asked for a bandage."

Grace looked at him curiously, but didn't interrupt.

"I asked her what it was for and she said that her mommy was bleeding, and she needed a bandage. I followed the little girl over to where her mother was slumped over in the corner of the room."

"Blood was trickling out of her ear, and her face was ashen white. Her little brother lay in a small stroller, and I don't think he could've been more than three months old at the time," he said.

"What happened to her?" Grace asked with shock in her voice.

"She'd taken her kids and fled her home. Her husband had beaten on her so badly that they barely made it to the soup kitchen before she died from being hit in the head several times by his fists."

Grace shook her head in disbelief. "This is incredible. That poor woman. Those poor kids."

Charles blew out a sigh. "I took the kids into the back of the kitchen and gave the little girl something to eat and had one of the women fill the baby's bottle and feed him as I called 911."

Grace put her arm around Charles's shoulder and ran her fingers through the back of his hair. His eyes closed, and he breathed deeply.

"What happened to the two kids?" Grace asked.

"After I called the police, I called my parents to come down to the kitchen. They arrived just as the police were about to call children's aid to have them come and pick up the kids."

Your parents took the kids?" Grace asked.

A smile formed on his lips and his eyes twinkled. "My mother couldn't have any more kids and she desperately wanted more. They convinced the police to let them take the kids."

"Wow!" Grace said in amazement. "That was so great of your parents to do that."

Charles pulled out his wallet from his jacket and flipped it open to a photo of a young woman and a teenage boy. "This is my sister Annie and my brother Steven," he said with pride.

"Your parents adopted them?" Grace was totally caught off guard.

He nodded with pride. "Annie is in her third year of university, and Steven is a straight A student in high school."

Grace was beginning to see a different side of Charles. It was a side of him that would make any parent proud to call him their son. She was finding herself falling for him which was unusual for Grace being they just met earlier that day.

"I'm finished my ice cream," grace whispered. "I guess this is the end of our date."

SEVEN

Becky felt her cheek burn as Joe slapped her again.

"Wake up, bitch!" he growled as he slapped her a third time.

She tried to cry out in pain, but her mouth was taped. She shivered and focused on her surroundings. Tears burned her eyes as she tried to move her body. She was tied to a table, and Joe was straddling her has he continued to slap her awake.

His body was sweaty, and he was naked from the waist up.

She blinked tears from her eyes and made a muffling cry as she felt Joe's hands on her naked and bruised body.

"Good. You're awake. Now we can have a little fun," he laughed menacingly as he unzipped his pants. "I hate to have you sleep through all the fun."

Becky looked around the room. It reminded her of a dark chamber in some horror film. The smell of dampness filled her nostrils. A window to the side was boarded up so the room wasn't visible to prying eyes.

But who would be prying on them? Joe's house was far from the main road and, unless someone knew what to look for, one would miss it completely.

Joe ripped the tape from Becky's mouth with one quick pull. The tape stung her mouth, and her dry lips bled as some of her skin was pulled off along with the tape. She could taste blood on her tongue as Joe lay on top of her and proceeded to attack her for the second time.

"Tell me you love it," he demanded.

Becky cried as he forced himself on her. "Please! I'll do what you ask. Just don't hurt me," she cried between sobs.

He slapped her again. "TELL ME YOU LOVE IT!" he screamed.

Becky cried in pain as he punched her hard in the mouth. "I love it," she said just before she blacked out again.

Grace sat straight up in bed. Charles was asleep beside her, and for a moment she forgot she wasn't alone. He moaned and rolled over, wrapping his arm around her waist.

Grace found herself breathing heavy and felt her lips. She tasted blood.

The clock read three a.m.

"What's wrong?" Charles asked with a groggy voice.

"I don't know," grace replied. "Something's happening." She grabbed her robe, slipped it on, and went into the living room.

Charles slipped on his boxers and followed. He watched as Grace sat on the sofa, allowing herself to go into a trance.

After a few minutes Grace came out of it. "We have to find the other one," she said. "She isn't dead yet but she's in a great deal of pain."

Charles sat beside Grace. "Do you have an idea where she is?' he asked.

Grace closed her eyes again and shook her head. "Henry keeps telling me about a dungeon in a castle which makes no sense."

"Can he see the people?"

Once again Grace shook her head. "It's too dark in the dungeon for him to make out their faces. All he hears is the girl crying."

"Tell him to turn on a light, for christsake!" Charles insisted.

Grace opened her eyes. "Henry told me to tell you that he's a spirit guide and not a bloody poltergeist. He can't just walk over to the wall and flip on a switch."

Grace blew out a sigh. "Great! Now you've pissed him off."

"Tell him I'm sorry. This is my first time dealing with a spirit guide," he said.

"I'll tell him in the morning." Grace yawned. "There's nothing we can do for now."

"I don't think I can sleep now, knowing there's another girl out there being attacked by this sick bastard," he said.

Grace understood how he was feeling but over the years she learned that it was best to keep her emotions at arm's length when dealing with information that Henry brought to her.

"You need to let go." Grace said. "I know it's difficult but there's nothing we can do. We need to continue and keep the information that we do get from Henry, in the back of our minds."

"How can you easily dismiss this?" he asked.

"Do you honestly think that I'm just dismissing it? Do you know how many times Henry's given me information that's disturbing? Half the time the information is a past memory of his that he's reliving. This could be one of those times."

"I'm sorry," Charles said. "All this spirit stuff is new to me. I have no clue what's real and what isn't."

Grace slipped her hand in his. "Everything that Henry tells me is real. The problem is that I never know if it's one of his memories or if it's a present day event."

"How do you separate the two?"

Grace shrugged. "The fact that he's talking about a dungeon could mean that it's a past memory of his."

"How can you tell for sure?"

"You can't, but do you know where there's a dungeon around here?"

"Good point," Charles said.

"Well, aside from the wax museum on Clifton Hill and the haunted mansion on Lundy's Lane, I don't know of any," Grace added.

Grace gave out a yawn and stretched her arms.

"Maybe we should continue this conversation in the other room," Charles said as he pulled Grace from the sofa.

She fell into his arms, and he kissed her gently as he led her back to the bedroom. They once again had wild animal sex.

It wasn't like Grace to give herself so quickly to someone, but there was something about Charles that made Grace feel as if she could trust him. She couldn't quite pinpoint it but whatever it was it didn't hurt that he had the looks of a God and a body that could sink a ship.

She also felt that he wouldn't think of this as a one time-deal. His tenderness wasn't something that he could pretend.

He had genuine feelings for Grace and this as well as his great looks and rock hard body made it easy for her to have him in her bed.

Even if Charles thought of this as a one night stand, this didn't bother Grace. She was notorious for doing the exact same thing though university. It made life easier for her to not get emotionally attached to anyone.

But she was older now, and she had thoughts of finding someone on a one to one basis. Was Charles the one to fill that role?

Could Grace take him into her life as easily? Grace's life was complicated, and she had devoted so much time to her work. What also lingered in the back of her mind was the thought of committing to him.

Grace's grandmother as well as her mother never committed themselves to the men in their lives. This was obvious since they never married the man who was the father of their only child. Was Grace to follow in their footsteps?

What if Charles was the man that her mother and grandmother spoke about? The man who was to be the father of her only daughter? Maybe Grace should just take one step at a time. After all, he may not be the man. He may just be one of the men who would come and go from her life and she was quite happy having him in her life for the moment.

The sex was fantastic and he taught her a few sexy moves between the sheets. She could get used to this jungle sex with Charles.

"What are you thinking about?" Charles asked as he kissed Grace's neck, then her lips.

Their eyes met and she gently brushed his blond hair from his face. "Jungle sex," she whispered.

Grace stood at the back door watching Charles pull out the back lot. They made a date to see each other later after work. He said he'd try to swing by Clifton Hill around noon to say hello, and bring lunch.

Once his car disappeared around the corner, Grace closed the door and went to shower and dress for her day on the Hill.

Grace tied her black hair back with a bright red scarf and lined her eyes with the usual thick eyeliner and mascara. If she were to convince people of her authenticity, she had to look the part of a gypsy fortune teller. She picked out a long cotton skirt with a yellow tee.

The weather had cooled slightly from the rain the day before, so she brought along a thick red shawl just in case there was no chance of warming up.

Grace almost made a quick getaway before being stopped by the sound of the back door opening and closing.

"So tell us what happened last night," her mother asked as she and granny made their way across the back lot to Grace's car.

"Since when have you known me to kiss and tell?" Grace said shyly.

They looked at each other and grinned.

"See, I told you he'd stay," Granny said to mom. "You owe me ten dollars."

Love and Murder on the Hill

Grace stood there with her hands on her hips as she watched the money exchange hands.

"Are you saying that you both bet on whether I was going to have him stay the night or not?"

"Well it didn't start out that way," mom said. "It kinda just happened."

Grace slammed the trunk closed and crossed her arms in disbelief. "What do you mean it just kinda happened? How does that sort of thing just kinda happen?"

"Well, your mother told me that you wouldn't allow this man to stay over, and I disagreed. I said you were a woman of the new century, and if the two of you hit it off, you'd definitely take advantage of it," Granny said.

Grace put her hands to her ears as she did many times when it came to her family discussing her life. "I don't need to hear anymore. I'm going to work, and when I get back, I don't want to hear another word about my sex life or lack thereof."

Grace got in her car, revved the engine, and waved to the two women as she whipped her car out of the lot and headed for the tourist area of town.

Sarah was at her desk when Charles strolled into the office. "Where have you been? I've been trying to reach you all night," she said.

"Sorry, I had plans last night and didn't want to be disturbed," he replied as he took his place behind his desk that sat across from Sarah's.

"I wish I knew that," she said. "Another girl is missing."

Charles stopped what he was doing and gave Sarah his undivided attention. "Tell me."

"A couple from the States came in reporting their eighteen-year-old daughter missing. She left while they were asleep." Sarah said.

"How do they know she just didn't go sightseeing?" he asked.

Sarah shook her head. "That's what they thought, too, so they waited till later on to call. But they kept calling her cell phone, and she wasn't picking up."

Sarah handed the typed report to Charles to read over. "They came in late last night in a panic that their daughter hadn't tried to get in touch with them."

Charles studied the photo of the young woman. "She looks older than eighteen," he said.

"I think she may have met someone the day before. She might be shacked up in some room."

"Or she might be with this serial killer we have running around," Charles added.

Sarah nodded. "I have a feeling that this may be the case, too, but I don't want to believe that yet." Sarah grabbed her jacket. "We better go talk to who was at the front desk when she left."

EIGHT

Grace had already finished six full readings by the time noon rolled around. As usual mom showed up to collect her earnings and to relieve Grace so she could stretch her legs, use the washroom or grab some food.

"Charles said he was going to try and swing by and bring lunch," Grace said with hope in her voice.

A wide toothy smile filled mom's face. "He's such a nice man. I'm happy that you're finally dating."

Grace rolled her eyes. "Mom, it was only one date, and I don't think that would be considered dating."

She waved her hand at her daughter like she always did when she wanted to dismiss anything Grace had to say. "The first of many," she said.

"I'm glad you have more confidence in this than I do."

She sat with Grace another fifteen minutes, then finally had to leave. Although there weren't as many people walking the streets as the other day, this didn't slow Grace's business down at all. She always had a full list of people waiting to hear good news of the future.

Her readings consisted of two prices. Thirty dollars for a tarot reading of the past, present and future and for an extra ten dollars, she would do a palm reading. Most clients chose the forty dollar value of the full reading.

Grace checked her watch after three more readings and glanced up and down the street. No Charles.

It was going on three, and within minutes the sky went from bright blue to black. Lightening was seen in the distance and ten seconds later was followed by the sound of thunder.

"Time to pack up," Grace mumbled.

Charles had failed to show, and Grace was feeling a bit slighted. Aaron and Marco were packing up for the night as the rain started to come down.

Grace hoisted her umbrella, gathered her things, and got everything safely tucked in the trunk of her car just as it down poured.

People were running for cover in all directions as Grace slowly pulled her car out of the parking lot and merged with the traffic on Clifton Hill.

She was feeling hurt and abandoned as she drove the distances to her house.

She parked her car in the lot behind her apartment. Instead of going up the stairs, Grace crossed the lot and ran the distance between her house and the adult shop next door.

"I need something to cheer me up," Grace said barging through the door.

Sue, who was on the ladder busy arranging merchandise, almost fell off when Grace came in. "Damn it, girl! You scared the shit out of me. Didn't you see me up here?"

"Oops, sorry. Should I come in again?" Grace asked sarcastically.

Sue climbed down the ladder and rearranged her tight leather skirt. "That attitude will get you bitch-slapped one of these days."

Grace picked up a couple of movies and read the caption on them. "Sorry. I'm just in a mood today." she sighed.

"You need something to get you in another mood?" she asked as she saw her friend reading the DVDs.

Grace put them back on the counter. "Don't need to be in that kind of mood. I had my fill of that last night," she said.

"Oh, do tell, girl!" Sue asked with excitement.

Grace's mood changed as she remembered her reason for coming in. "It was great, but he stood me up today."

"That dirty bastard!" Sue said in Grace's defense.

"That's okay. It's not like we had a date carved in stone. He said he'd try to swing by with lunch today."

Sue thought for a moment, then a light went off in her gothic head. "Don't tell me you did that gorgeous cop from yesterday?" She put her hand over her black colored lips. Her nail polish matched her makeup.

Grace gave her a smile and nodded.

"Oh, my God! I just knew it. You have that fresh look of satisfaction on your face," she squealed. "You have to tell me everything!"

"Maybe later. For now I'd rather just savor last night with him, to myself."

"Okay, okay. But when you're finished savoring, you better tell me everything, and don't leave anything out.

"So why are you bummed out now?" Sue asked.

"I don't know. Maybe I'm being too sensitive."

"If he said he was going to try and swing by, that isn't really what I would call a commitment to meeting up," Sue said.

Grace nodded in agreement. "You're right. He's a cop so something might have come up."

Grace sat on the chair behind the counter and watched Sue rearrange the merchandise on the shelves.

"I wish for once that when customers pick up an item to look at , would put it back in the same spot. Or at least in the same general area. Look at this," she said, calling Grace over.

Grace walked over to where Sue was standing with her hands on her hips. "Can you believe this?"

Grace looked over at the shelves, but couldn't make hide nor hair of what she was talking about.

Half the things in the store left Grace scratching her head over for what they were used for, and the other half just simply scared the hell out of her.

She picked up a rubber dolphin from a stack that resembled a heavy rubber ring. "This is for women, and these are for men. As if some of this shit isn't confusing enough. Do I need customers coming in here and buying the wrong thing for themselves?" She placed the dolphin in its proper place and walked back to the counter. Grace followed closely.

The door buzzed and in walked Charles. Grace felt her heart jump into her throat and her thighs start to quiver as he strolled over and gave Grace a kiss on the cheek.

"I'm so sorry about not being able to make it for lunch," he apologized. "I got tied up with a missing persons report."

"You're forgiven," Grace said with a smile.

He picked up one of the videos that was still sitting on the counter. "Are you buying these?" he asked curiously. "Have slut, will travel," he read out loud.

Grace's face flushed. "No! Sue forgot to put them on the shelf."

He pulled out his wallet. "Why don't we buy it anyway so we can watch it together?" He grinned.

Grace wasn't sure if he was serious or just yanking her chain.

"Hell, if you want a couple's movie, let me suggest sandwich gang bang," Sue said. She went to the DVD section of the store and returned a moment later with movie in hand.

"You're joking, right?" Grace asked, half panicking and half jokingly.

"I never joke when it comes to good quality porn."

"MY feelings exactly." Sue added.

Charles handed Sue his Visa.

"Gold card, eh?" Sue commented as she took the card. "Maybe I can interest you in some of our finer merchandise to use during and after the movie."

"No!" Grace shrieked. "The movie is more than enough."

Ten minutes later they were watching couples doing the dirty deed in a velvet draped room. There were five couples in all, and every so often they would get too close and start helping themselves to the couple next to each other.

Grace kept turning her head sideways to try and make sense of whose legs belonged to whom.

"Do couples really do these sorts of things?" she asked, not really sure if she wanted an answer.

"Seeing that sex parties are legal in Ontario, I wouldn't be surprised if they do," he replied. His eyes were fixed on the screen, and Grace could have sworn he was foaming at the mouth.

"Is this stuff turning you on?" she asked curiously.

He turned to look at her, and he had that deer in the headlights look. "What makes you think that?"

Love and Murder on the Hill

"Well, for one thing, you're all red in the face as if you just ran a marathon." Grace laughed. "And secondly, you're panting."

He raised his hands and laughed out loud. "Guilty as charged."

Grace moved closer to him. "I could help you calm down a little." Her tongue circled his neck, and she gently tugged on his earlobe with her mouth.

Charles flipped off the television. "A repeat of last nights performance?"

Twenty minutes later they fell in a heap on the sofa. Grace's sofa hadn't seen so much action since the guy came in and cleaned it.

"I'd carry you into the bedroom but my knees are weak, and I would be afraid of dropping you," he whispered between deep breaths.

"I never had sex on a sofa before let alone raw monkey sex," she said laying her head on his shoulder.

Grace closed her eyes as he wrapped his arms around her. She felt safe in his arms and never wanted the feeling to end.

It had been a long time since Grace felt a man's arms around her. Not that she didn't have any offers, Grace just knew that they wouldn't have made her feel more wanted and more secure than Charles made her feel that moment.

Charles opened his eyes and stared down at Grace. "Monkey sex?"

Joe untied Becky so she could wash up. He led her to a partly renovated bathroom that had an olive green bathtub and toilet on a bare plywood floor. The bathroom had seen better days and was in dire need of a good cleaning. Joe ran the water in the tub and ordered Becky to wash herself up.

"Will you let me go after this?" she asked, begging.

"Of course I'll let you go," Joe said with a smile. "When I'm finished with you."

He closed the door and locked it, and his laughter could be heard in the other room.

Becky relieved herself, then slowly climbed into the water.

It stung at first as she inched her bruised and battered body down in the water, but eventually felt good.

She took the bar of soap that Joe provided for her and scrubbed her body clean, trying to wash any scent of her captor from her.

She whimpered and cried thinking of her situation and what she had endured the past few days.

He seemed so nice when she met him. He gave her so much attention. How could she have been so naive and just meet up with him without telling her parents?

Her parents! She thought. They must be going crazy wondering where she was. Tears burned her eyes as she thought about her parents. She wondered if she would ever see them again.

She knew in her heart that Joe wasn't going to let her go. Why would he? She knew too much, and it was obvious that if she were let free, she'd definitely go to the police.

He had made no attempt to hide his identity or where he lived from her. Panic set in as she thought about her demise. She knew she had to do something. She had to at least try to survive.

Charles met Sarah for coffee before they started work. "Any word on the missing girl?" he asked.

She shook her head and ordered a latte with extra cream. "No news so far."

Charles ordered the same. "I think this is beginning to smell like another victim."

They took a seat near the window so they could people watch as they sipped their hot drinks.

"One thing is that this girl was reported missing the first day. At least we have a time frame of her disappearance if we find her in the same state as the other bodies," Sarah said.

"Let's pray that won't the case," Charles said with a heavy sigh.

"We've tried her cell phone, but no luck," Sarah said.

Sarah removed her black blazer and hung it on the back of her chair. She fanned herself with a napkin as the morning sun filled the coffee shop with early morning warmth.

"It's going to be a nice day," Charles said, as he turned his seat to avoid direct contact with the brightness.

"So where have you been going to these past few nights?" Sarah asked, changing the subject.

Charles gave a secret grin from ear to ear. "I'm not one to kiss and tell," he said shyly.

This peaked Sarah's curiosity as well her green eyed monster.

She'd had a secret crush on her new partner since they were first assigned together and even though she'd thrown subtle hints his way, he never seemed to bite. Now he was involved with someone else, and although she was just plain curious to know who she was, she secretly wanted to rip the girl's hair out.

She undid a couple of buttons on her white shirt to reveal some cleavage.

"Oh, come, on." she insisted slightly leaning over the table to give Charles a view. "If you can't tell your partner, then who can you tell?" Charles drank the rest of his coffee, ignoring her question and her cleavage. "All I can say is thank you for that suggestion the other night."

Sarah sat back in her chair and eyed her partner, feeling slightly rejected.

Charles gathered the empty cups and napkins and disposed of them in the recycle bin.

Sarah followed Charles out the door. "Please don't tell me you're interested in Grace the psychic?" she asked with slight sarcasm in her voice.

Charles opened Sarah's car door for her. "What's wrong with Grace? I find her quite interesting and beautiful," he said defensively.

Sarah shrugged, and slid behind the wheel of her car. "If you're into that sort of distorted life, then by all means go for it."

Charles moved back from the car and put his hand in his pockets to retrieve his keys. "Why do I sense a 'but' here?"

"No buts. I just believe you should rethink getting serious with her. Her mother and grandmother are crazy, and Grace isn't too far behind them in the sanity department."

"Thanks for your concern but I'm a big boy and can take care of myself," he said with a wink and a smile.

"Indeed you can." Sarah revved the engine, put the car in drive and pulled out of the parking lot, leaving Charles in the dust.

"What the hell was that all about?" he said out loud.

NINE

Joe walked into the bathroom where he left his prisoner to clean herself up. Becky tried her best to hide her naked body with the dirty towel that she used to dry herself.

He had a piece of bungee cord in his hand. "You shouldn't be so shy around me," he said as he pulled the towel from her.

Becky whimpered as she tried to cover her bruised, naked body with her hands. Tears stung her eyes. "Please," she begged. "Please let me go home to my parents."

Joe ignored her pleas as he moved closer until Becky could feel his hot breath on her face.

She submissively lowered her head. Annoyed by this, Joe grabbed her hair and snapped her head back to force her to look at him.

She cried out in pain. "Please, I won't tell anyone. I'll tell my parents that I met up with someone, and we took off for a few days."

Joe was getting more annoyed by her useless pleas. "Shut up bitch!" His voice was dark and wild as he pushed her to her knees.

Becky whimpered as her battered body trembled.

"You're totally useless to me, bitch. Your annoying pleas and your constant crying is boring the shit out of me. And you can't do one simple thing to keep my interest.

He took the cord that he was still holding and tied Becky's hands behind her back. He then led her back into the other room and laid her back on the table, tying each ankle as he had done before.

Becky pleaded with her captor. "Please let me go. I promise I won't tell anyone about you or where you live." Tears rolled down the sides of her face as her arms ached being tied behind her.

Joe ignored her, and moved towards her head.

Becky felt his hand brush her hair away from her face. For a brief moment it felt soothing.

Thoughts of her father and mother touching her head before she fell asleep, flooded her thoughts. But this person wasn't her parents. This person had no desire to protect her. His only goal was to satisfy his sexual perversions by doing whatever he wanted with her.

Joe took a roll of duct tape and used his teeth to rip a piece off.

He placed it over Becky's mouth. He ripped another piece, but decided that this time he wasn't going to tape his victim's nose as he had done previously.

Dread filled her as she felt the plastic bag go over her head and the duct tape seal off any air.

Becky squirmed to free herself as she gasped for air. The cord cut into her ankles as she tried to kick her legs free. Her shoulder dislocated as she moved frantically trying to pull her hands free from behind her.

She could see Joe's distorted face inches from the plastic as if he wanted to see the life leave her eyes.

He was studying her with curiosity as Becky's struggling slowed, and her body became lifeless.

"Now you can go," Joe moaned as if pleased to grant Becky's wish.

He kissed Becky's forehead through the plastic bag, then left the room, flicking the lights off behind him.

"I'll get rid of you later," he said as he left her body alone in the dark on the cold dirty table.

Grace was washing dishes when she was suddenly overcome with the feeling of a presence. Grace turned to see a young woman standing in front of her. She was slightly transparent, indicating she was from beyond this world.

Grace watched her for a moment as she stood there before her. "What can I do for you?" Grace calmly asked.

She seemed startled at her surroundings and of her request. She didn't respond.

Grace called upon the help of Henry, her connection to the spirit world.

"Please tell her she must move on," Grace told Henry.

"She has a message for you," Henry said. "She wants you to tell her parents that she's sorry and that she loves them very much."

Grace felt tears form in her eyes. She blinked as they fell down her face. Grace had seen this girl before, but couldn't place her.

Her head nodded in agreement as Henry told her that she was in the spirit world and needed to move on through the tunnel and not to be afraid. As it became apparent to Grace who she was, the spirit vanished as suddenly as she appeared.

"Ask her who killed her," Grace said to Henry.

"Too late, Miss Grace. She's moved on," Henry said.

"Damn," Grace stammered. "Damn, damn, damn."

"Miss Grace, you shouldn't use that word. You're a lady and ladies don't cuss," Henry said before he, too, disappeared.

Joe made himself some lunch and settled on the living room sofa. He flipped on the television just as Becky's parents were pleading for whoever held their daughter or whoever has any knowledge of her whereabouts, to please contact the Niagara Falls Police Department.

They held a recent photo of their daughter, and it was enlarged on the screen just before Joe switched channels to Jerry Springer.

He laughed as he took a bite of his sandwich. "I'll see to it that you get her back soon."

Grace watched the news as Becky's photo was splashed across the screen. The hairs on the back of her neck stood to attention as she saw the face of the girl who was in her kitchen moments ago. Her heart felt heavy for her parents who still held onto hope that their daughter would be alive.

Grace knew that it was a hope that would never be realized. Their daughter was dead, and the only thing they had to look towards is their daughters' funeral.

Grace picked up the phone and made a call to Charles.

"Detective Richmond."

"She's dead." Grace sighed deeply.

Charles went momentarily silent. "Who's dead?"

"Becky." Grace sobbed.

"How do you know this?"

"Her spirit visited me."

"I'll be right over," he said.

Grace held the phone in her hand and cried.

Twenty minutes later Charles was holding Grace in his arms, comforting her. He'd made a quick stop at Timmy's and brought Grace a small green tea. He seemed to think that it would help her, and he was right.

In a short time, he knew more about Grace than people who'd known her for years. She liked that.

"Are you feeling a little better?" he asked in a calm voice.

Grace nodded. "I'm glad you're here, and thanks for the tea."

"Do you feel up to telling me what you were talking about on the phone?"

She nodded again. "Sometimes when people have passed on, their spirits will visit someone who's sensitive to the spirit world. It's happened to me before, but not when it involved a missing person."

Charles sat silently, allowing Grace to continue.

"I was washing my dishes and felt her presence. I turned, and she was standing there."

"How do you know it was her?" he asked.

"At first I didn't. I called Henry to speak to her and tell her that she's passed on and that she needed to move on through the tunnel. It wasn't until after she'd moved on that I realized I'd seen her face before."

"Did you try to get any information from her?"

Grace shook her head. "By the time I realized who she was, it was too late. She'd already moved on."

"Damn," Charles said.

"That's exactly what I said," Grace replied.

"If she's another victim and has been murdered, then he'll try to dispose of the body."

"I was thinking the same thing, but the problem is where will he drop her body?" Grace asked.

Probably the same place as his last victims. Somewhere along the shores of the Niagara River."

"You'll have to watch the shore but that's going to be a problem since you're not sure if she's another victim and given the length of the river, where would you start?" Grace said.

Grace thought for a moment. "Charles, I'm no detective, but from what I've seen on cop shows, wouldn't victims of serial killers usually have something in common?"

"Yes, in some cases. But we're still trying to piece that together."

"I'd like to look at the photos and info on the girls, if that would be okay. Maybe a new set of eyes would see something that others wouldn't."

Charles kissed Grace on the cheek. "You see things that others wouldn't see all the time." He smiled.

Grace rolled her eyes at him. "Are you trying to get romantic with me?"

He sat back and tried to put on his most innocent face. "Me? I wouldn't hear of it!"

A devilish smile formed on his lips. "But if you want to, it's not above me to oblige."

Grace blew out a sigh. She still had sore muscles from the last time he obliged. "Is that all men think about?"

Charles thought for a moment. "No. we think about other things, too, like football, pizza and body gas."

Grace shook her head in disbelief. "Maybe it would have helped if I had a brother so I could understand men."

"We aren't complicated people. Just give us food, sex, and a remote and we're pretty much set for life."

"I'll make a note of that." She laughed trying to forget her reason for having him there.

Marco was sweet-talking a bunch of young teenagers while Aaron was helping a couple climb the rock wall when Grace took a break from reading.

The weather had turned mild again, and the Hill was quickly filling with people.

It'd been over a week since Becky had disappeared, and her body had yet to be found. Grace had tried to contact her again through Henry, with no success. It was always difficult when they've moved on through the tunnel, especially when the person was a new spirit.

Grace watched as Marco took the phone numbers of one of the young giggling girls and made a promise to call. He tossed the number in the trash can once the girls disappeared in the crowd on Clifton Hill.

Grace shook her head in disgust just as his attention was turned in her direction. He crossed the alleyway and plopped himself down across from Grace.

"Sorry, Marco, the chair's for customers only," she said, leaning back and crossing her arms.

He took two twenties out of his pocket and slapped it on the table. "I'm a customer. I want a reading." He took the cards and started to shuffle them.

Grace tried to take them from him, but he was determined to get a reading from her. "Okay, fine. Just don't try anything."

Grace told him the procedure, and took the cards from him. "Did you make your wish?" she asked as she laid five cards out on the table.

He nodded and grinned.

Grace sighed, knowing very well what his wish may be. "If you wished about getting into my pants, the only way it'll happen is if I threw them out and you picked them up to try them on."

His smile faded. "I wouldn't waste a good wish on that. I already know you won't go out with me."

He was definitely right about that. He'd never asked for a reading before, and she thought this was a perfect opportunity to make him sweat.

Marco flirted with anything with breasts and never once thought of the consequences to his callous actions.

"So Miss, Fortune Teller, what do you see in my future?" he asked nonchalantly.

Grace looked over his cards and squinted in disbelief. "Are you sure you want me to tell you what I see in your future?" she asked with hesitation.

"I paid my money, and I want a reading."

Grace sighed deeply. "Okay, but don't complain if I tell you something you don't like."

"I see several women in your near future. One will be giving you something," Grace said.

"Oh, this sounds great! Can you see what she'll be giving me?"

Grace pointed to the middle card. "It looks as if it's some type of illness. You'll be getting sick," she continued.

His smile dropped from his face and his olive complexion turned pale green.

"Are you saying that some bitch is going to give me some S.T.D.?"

"Yep. Looks about the size of it," Grace replied, trying to keep a straight face. "You're using protection, I hope."

He sat silent, thinking over how to answer the question. "Well, some of them insist I go without it. They always assure me there's nothing wrong with them and that they're on birth control," he said.

"And you believe them?" grace asked.

He didn't respond.

Grace shook her head. "You're old enough to know better, Marco," she scolded. "First of all, you shouldn't be so promiscuous, and second, you should never, and I mean never, have unprotected sex."

"Okay fine. I'll start taking precautions. What else do the cards say?" he asked.

Grace did a mental eye roll. That didn't seem to faze him, she thought. She looked over the cards again. "I see a man coming to you," Grace said.

"Is this a good thing?" he asked.

She shook her head. "He's angry and big."

"You mean fat?" he asked.

She shook her head again. "I mean body building type. Tall and muscular."

Marco seemed puzzled. "Why's he angry, and what does he want with me?"

Grace's eyes gazed up at his face. Was he for real? she thought. Does she really need to spell this out to him?

"It seems you're going to have a relationship with his girlfriend or sister. Someone close to him. Anyway, you pass on this illness or get this person pregnant, and you just walk away."

Grace could have sworn she heard Marco shudder.

"Is he going to beat me up?" he asked.

"It kind of goes black after that. I don't know the answer," Grace replied.

"It goes black? What the hell do you mean that it goes black?"

Grace gathered the cards. "All I can tell you is that the outcome is determined on your behavior from this moment on."

Marco narrowed his eyes. "Are you telling me the true or are you shitting me?"

Grace ignored his question and handed him the cards.

She asked him to shuffle them before he had time to think if she was pulling his leg or not. "Cut them into three piles, then pick a pile."

He did so and waited patiently for Grace to turn up the cards.

"Do you have a question for me that I can answer yes or no to?" Grace asked.

"Will I be cured of this illness?" he asked without hesitation.

Grace flipped over a card. "Yes but it'll take a long time before you're even aware that you have it."

"I thought you asked me for a question that you can answer yes or no to?" He was becoming suspicious.

"And you did. I answered you with a yes, but the cards were showing more. That happens sometimes," Grace assured him.

"Will I become rich with my business?" he asked.

Grace nodded. "But you need to control your spending and look to invest your money in other endeavors."

"One more question," Grace said.

"Will you ever go out with me?" he asked, catching her off guard.

"No, that will never happen," Grace replied without hesitation.

"Hey, you never turned a card over," he shouted.

Grace flipped a card over without looking at it. "There you go. And it still says you have a snowball's chance in hell of getting me to go out with you."

TEN

It was just past seven by the time Grace pulled into the back lot. Charles phoned her earlier to say he won't be able to come over tonight because of the search for Becky.

Grace was too tired to see him anyway and told him not to worry. Grace was getting the feeling that she somehow managed to get herself into a relationship without even knowing it.

Grace showered and washed her face free of makeup. She towel-dried her hair and tied it back into a damp ponytail. She slipped on her most comfortable flannel pajamas and flipped through the several take-out menus that were stashed in her kitchen junk drawer.

After some thought, Grace settled on Chinese and ordered enough to feed an army. It was a bad habit, but she knew in two hours she'd be hungry again.

Grace settled on the sofa with remote in hand and flipped through the channels until she found a good movie to keep her attention.

Her food arrived, and she pigged out on a large plate of Chinese while washing it down with a frosty beer.

A knock at her door made Grace jump. She checked my watch. It was past eleven. "Who'd be at my door at this time?" Grace wondered.

She peeked out the kitchen window and saw a woman standing on her porch stoop. She looked familiar, but Grace couldn't place her. Then it came to her. She's the mother of the missing girl.

Grace opened the door slightly and peered out at her. "Can I help you?" she asked.

"Are you the fortune teller?"

"That would all depend on which one you're looking for."

The woman pulled her sweater closed as a gust of wind pushed on Grace's door and sent chills down her spine. Not a good sign, grace thought.

"There's more than one of you?"

"My grandmother and mother are also fortune tellers, but if you're looking for the one who reads fortunes in the tourist area then that would be me."

Her face lit up with relief. "I'm sorry to bother you. I was told by the fellow who runs the haunted mansion that I could find you here."

Grace opened the door for her. "Would you like to come in?"

She nodded and managed a smile as she slipped past Grace into the kitchen.

She rubbed her arms to remove any remnants of the cold from her body. "Is the weather always like this in Niagara Falls?" she asked, trying to make small talk.

"May's an unpredictable month when it comes to weather," Grace said.

Grace led her into the living room and motioned for her to sit. "Can I offer you a drink?"

"I don't usually drink alcohol, but I wouldn't mind a beer," she replied as she spotted the half empty bottle on the coffee table.

Grace went to the fridge and returned with an opened bottle of beer and a tall glass. She took the beer from her, ignored the glass, and took three gulps before speaking.

"Do you know why I'm here?" she asked as if testing Grace's abilities.

Grace nodded. "Your daughter Becky is missing. You think I can help you."

Her eyes widened and hope filled her face.

"I recognized your face from the news," Grace added.

"Of course," she said with disappointment.

Grace's heart went out to this woman. She knew her daughter was dead, but how could she tell her that? How could Grace crush her hopes of finding her daughter safe and sound?

"I heard that you're the real deal," she said.

"You might say that. I inherited my abilities from my mother, and she got them from her mother."

She picked at the label from her bottle and peeled it back slightly until it ripped in her hand. "They can't find my daughter."

Her voice cracked, and tears pooled in her eyes. She blinked twice, and tears ran freely down her face.

Grace wanted to reach out to her, but held herself firm. Grace didn't want to get emotionally attached to the case.

It is an unwritten law in her family of fortune tellers that they never read their own cards or get emotionally involved with any of the clients who have a family member in trouble. It makes it too difficult to focus on their abilities if their emotions are in the way.

"What do you think I can do for you?" Grace asked.

"Can you help me find my daughter?"

Grace shook her head. "I can't guarantee that my reading of your cards will give you any information."

"What about a séance? You do séances, don't you?" It's obvious she did her homework on Grace and her family.

"Séances are not my specialty. You'd have to ask my mother and grandmother about that."

She lowered her head and mumbled silently to herself. "What can I do? I can't just sit back while I wait for news on my daughter."

Grace picked up the phone and dialed her mother, waking her from a sound sleep. She explained the situation to her.

"Does she realize that the only way we could contact her daughter is if she's moved on to the other side?" mom asked.

"No," Grace replied, not wanting to upset the woman.

Mom became silent as Grace became uncomfortable.

"Have you talked to her daughter's spirit?" she finally asked.

Grace swallowed hard. "Yes, I have."

"We need to talk."

"Okay, but what should I tell her?"

"I would suggest telling her the truth, that her daughter is dead, but I don't think that's the reason why she's here to see you," Mom said. "Just tell her to come back tomorrow to talk to me. Maybe by then they'll find her daughter."

"My mother asked if you wouldn't mind coming back tomorrow during the day," Grace said, hanging up the phone.

Grace couldn't look the woman in the face.

"Do you know anything about my daughter?" she asked.

Grace lowered her head, avoiding the question. "Please come back tomorrow, and my mother and grandmother will try to help you."

Joe removed Becky's body from the bathtub. He scrubbed away as much evidence as he could. The river will get rid of the rest, he thought. He redressed her the way she arrived and carried her body up the stairs, laying her on the floor of his living room.

He went to his car and popped the trunk, then went to the back of the house where he kept a freezer chest. He removed a large block of ice that had two large rocks frozen inside. The block had two pieces of bungee cord frozen on each side. Half of the cords were sticking out the top and were long enough to firmly tie the body to the block of ice. When the ice melts, the cords would separate and be washed away.

Using a dolly, he transported the ice to the trunk, cords exposed on top.

He then retrieved Becky's body from the house and laid her face down on the block of ice. He covered the body with a tarp before closing the trunk.

He slipped behind the wheel and revved the engine.

"Two a.m.," he said, checking his watch. "It should be safe to dispose of the body. Not many people along the parkway at this time of night."

He pulled out of his long driveway and headed toward the edge of town where there was a boat launch near an undertow. He was well aware of this as he was once pulled under at the exact area when he was a child. He almost drowned if it weren't for some fast-thinking fishermen.

He thought his plans through carefully and calculated every step to ensure the body would be found miles from the drop off area. The frozen rocks would weigh the body down allowing it to be unseen on the surface.

The body would catch the current, and the weight of the ice would allow it to travel underwater until it reached its final destination. Once the ice melted the cords would wash away and no one would be the wiser. By this time the body would be miles downriver. Far from its original drop off location.

He drove cautiously down the parkway, making note of any traffic in the area. As usual, the road was deserted, and he felt confident that his plan would go as smoothly as the previous times. Besides, no one would be watching so far up from where his victims were found. The cops were too busy checking near the bottom of the falls to even fathom that they originated on the outskirts of town.

He pulled his car into the picnic area and cut his lights as he drove toward the boat launch. He backed his car down the launch area until the back of the car was inches from the water. He cut the engine, walked around to the back of the car, and popped the trunk.

Water was leaking from the melting ice, but he paid no attention. He removed the tarp and laid it out flat on the ground. He removed Becky's body and placed her on the ground. He then removed the block of ice and placed it on the tarp, then laid the body on top of the block. Joe carefully positioning her between the two bungee cords. He tied the cords tightly around her waist, then dragged the tarp down to the end of the boat launch.

Once part of the tarp was floating in the water, he pushed the block of ice off the tarp until it was fully engulfed with water. He used a long stick to carefully guide the block further out and watched as the undertow grabbed hold and pulled the ice and body beneath the current. He stood watching for a moment to make sure the ice didn't reappear on the surface.

Once he felt confident that everything was going as planned, he put the tarp back in the trunk, and drove back home.

"It'll take a couple of days before they find her." He laughed to himself. "Once again, I've proven myself smarter than the cops."

Grace woke up to Henry's voice in her head. "Henry, will you please let me sleep?" Grace muttered.

"You need to think about getting a boat," he insisted.

Grace yawned deeply. "What the heck are you talking about? And why would I want to get a boat?"

"If you had a boat, you could find the killer."

Grace put a pillow over her head to try to block out Henry, but it was no use. His voice was projected right to her mind, and nothing could block him out once he started talking.

"I don't understand getting a boat and finding the killer has to do with me."

He repeated his suggestion over and over.

"Okay, okay! I'll get a boat if you promise to let me sleep."

"Yes, maam," Henry answered, then his voice went quiet.

Grace closed her eyes, but it was too late. She was wide awake now. She dragged her body out of bed and headed for the bathroom. Grace stood in the shower for five minutes, allowing the water to bring her totally awake.

Twenty minutes later she was sipping tea in her kitchen, reading over the local paper. The disappearance of Becky was still headline news. Grace's heart pained as she recalled the visit with Becky's mother. She wishes she could give her hope, but she knew there was none.

The only thing Becky's parents could hope for now was to find their daughter's body so they could lay it to rest. But her spirit wouldn't rest until justice was served, and the only way for that to happen was to find her killer and prosecute him to the fullest extent of the law.

A knock on the door broke Grace's thoughts and made her jump.

"Good morning, sweetheart," Charles said as he greeted Grace with a bag of freshly baked cinnamon rolls and a kiss on the lips.

Her eyes glistened over. She wasn't quite sure if she was happier seeing his handsome face at her doorstep so early in the morning or the scent of fresh baked rolls.

He scooped Grace up in his arms and passionately pressed his lips against hers. Grace felt her toes curl and her thighs tighten as his lips moved from her mouth to her neck. Definitely seeing him, she thought to herself. The rolls were a close second.

"Are you always like this so early in the morning?" Grace asked after she came up for air.

He kissed her again with less force. "Only when I see you," he whispered.

Grace felt heat head straight to her private zone, and her legs turned to rubber. "Maybe we should eat these goodies you brought with you," she said, taking the bag from him.

Charles joined her at the kitchen table and bit into a warm cinnamon bun while she poured him a cup of coffee.

"What brings you here so early in the morning?" Grace asked.

"Aside from having breakfast with the new girl in my life, nothing."

"So I'm now considered the new girl in your life? When do I become the old girl in your life?"

Charles took a sip of his coffee. "Maybe when you're about sixty and we're retired in some tropical paradise for four months of the year."

"Sounds like a commitment to me," Grace laughed.

"Could be if you want it to be." He smiled his heart-stopping, southern zone heating, smile.

"How could I say no?" Grace responded.

They finished off the buns and drank the rest of the coffee. Grace cleared the table and loaded the dishes in the dishwasher. Normally she'd leave them in the sink until she ran out of clean plates and cups, and had no choice but to clean them.

Since meeting Charles, she's become more domesticated and neater. He brought out the best in her and some new things she never knew existed.

"Has the police had any luck in finding the missing girl yet?" Grace asked, as she flipped on the dishwasher.

"We haven't found Becky yet," he said with concern in his voice.

Grace was overwhelmed with sympathy for him and Becky's parents, as she noticed the pain in his face. This case disturbed him, and Grace knew that he hoped she could help him more than she had. Then Grace thought about the words Henry spoke to her early this morning.

Grace repeated Henry's words to Charles in hope to get some feedback on what the spirit might have meant.

"Do you think it's possible that the killer was dropping the bodies somewhere up river?" Grace asked.

"It's possible, but how could the body travel as far as it did without it being seen before the falls?"

"What if he weighed it down?" Grace asked.

He shook his head. "Even with an undertow, the body wouldn't travel that far being weighed down. Besides, there was nothing tied to the bodies when they were found."

They were at a dead end. There was no evidence that the bodies were dropped where they were found. On the contrary, the evidence showed that the bodies were in the water for some time, so they had to have been dumped somewhere up river. But how could he do this without anyone seeing him? One thing was for sure. The killer needed to be caught before there was another victim.

ELEVEN

Mom and granny were busy getting ready for the day when Grace strolled in the back door.

"Is Becky's mother coming today?" Grace asked, swiping a freshly baked cookie from the plate they left out for customers.

Granny and mom always tried to make people feel comfortable when they browsed the store. They always had homemade cookies and fresh coffee readily available to anyone who walked through the door. This also helped sales as people were more inclined to buy something when the place smelled like chocolate chip cookies.

Over the years they developed a cult following of regulars who'd come in to buy crystals or potions. They'd line up for a reading to see what their future held. Because of their uncanny accuracy, they built a positive position in the area.

Unfortunately, this didn't happen until Grace was in university. If it happened sooner, Grace might have had happier childhood memories. But she didn't hold it against them. They were great role models and loved Grace unconditionally, even though there were times when Grace was younger that she wished for a more normal family.

For a brief time during Grace's early teenage years, she resented their way of life. Grace was lonely and bitter and hated the life she had. She was never asked out on dates, never invited to parties or sleepovers. The only true friends she had were her mother and grandmother, and Grace hated to be around them.

They seemed to understand that and tried their best to give Grace her own space so she could find herself. She eventually came full circle and ended up being just like them. It was something that she was proud of, and Grace regrets ever wanting to break free of their lifestyle.

They greeted Grace with a kiss, and granny poured her a cup of hot chocolate to take the chill off. It was almost June, yet the cold hadn't let up. The sun was bright and welcoming but the winter chill still remained.

"She'll be by at closing time," Mom replied. "Will you be joining us?"

Grace raised her hands and took a step back. "I don't want to get involved with this one," she answered.

Granny took Grace's hand. "Grace, Becky has been in touch with you from beyond the grave. She has a connection with you. You have a better chance of being the line of communication between mother and daughter than your mom and me."

Grace took a deep breath. "Okay, fine. I'll be here." Granny always had a way of knocking down Grace's defenses. She just needed to make physical contact by touching her hand and she'd turn to pudding.

"Maybe you can ask that nice man to join us," She suggested.

"I don't know if he'd be interested in this sort of thing."

Grace noticed mom and granny winking at each other and that sent a red flag flying high. "What are you two up to?" Grace asked suspiciously.

"Oh, nothing," Mom said with a smile.

"It doesn't seem like nothing. What's going on here?"

Granny patted Grace's hand again. "Don't worry about it. Just enjoy being with Charles. He's perfect for you."

Grace wanted to pick their brains a little more on the subject, but decided to leave it for another time.

She was in no mood to have anyone put a damper on the relationship developing between her and Charles. He's the best thing that came into Grace's life in a long time, and she had no desire to lose it. At least not for the moment.

Thirty minutes later Grace was looking through the wigs at the shop next door.

"Something on your mind?" Sue asked as she handed Grace another wig for inspection.

"Why would you ask that?" Grace asked nonchalantly.

Love and Murder on the Hill

"I've come to realize that, when you have something on your mind, which is almost every time you come in here, you go through the wigs without trying one on."

Grace put the long red-haired wig back on the plastic head. "Am I that readable?"

She gave her friend a nod and a smile. "Don't worry about it," Sue said as she wrapped her arm around Grace's shoulder. "My business is similar to yours. I've learned to read people."

Grace found herself believing what Sue said. It made even more sense since Grace had been coming into the store the past few years to chat and try on wigs.

"So why don't you tell me what's eating you?" Sue asked.

Grace crossed her arms over her chest and joined Sue behind the counter. Grace told her about Becky and her mother. She told her about Charles and how things were moving so fast between them.

"My family's holding a séance tonight and I don't feel comfortable about being there."

"If you want, I can sit in for moral support," Sue said.

"You'll do that?"

"Sure I would. We're friends and, if this thing is going to be uncomfortable for you, the least I can do is be there for you."

Grace gave Sue a hug and thanked her for her friendship. "If there's anything I can do for you, don't hesitate to ask," Grace said.

Sue thought for a moment before speaking. "Well, there is one thing I could use," she said.

"Name it," Grace said without hesitation.

"My life is pretty boring since I'm between boyfriends. Would you mind doing a reading for me to see if I have anyone new coming into my life soon?"

"I thought you were seeing some gothic guy you met online."

She shrugged. "I was, but he was just a Goth wannabe."

"Who wants to be a Goth wannabe?"

"You'd be surprised." She laughed.

"It'd be my pleasure. Come over to my apartment after work. We can order some food, and I'll give you the full fortune telling treatment before we go to the séance."

"You got a date, girl," Sue said with a smile.

The friends chatted about life and love and how Charles makes Grace's body heat up twenty degrees every time he smiles. They talked about travelling and how Sue had dreams of going to Transylvania to see Dracula's castle.

"I heard it was for sale," Sue said enthusiastically. "Wouldn't it be wild to buy that place and turn it into a party hotel for lovers of the weird and mysterious?"

"Sounds like a great place to hold séances." Grace laughed.

"Yeah. I could decorate the place in traditional gothic, and you and your mom and granny could set up fortune telling booths and maybe hold a séance the last night for all the guests," Sue added.

It was a wild idea, but that was all it would be.

Some of Grace's ancestors were from around that area. The men had a habit of leaving a little of themselves in every town they came across. Maybe this was another reason why her grandmother and mother never married.

Grace checked her watch and was surprised that they'd been chatting for two hours.

"I better get going," Grace said, stretching her body after sitting for so long.

"I'll be over just after six," Sue said, giving Grace a hug.

Grace hugged her back and headed out the front door into the suddenly overcast weather. The sky was steel grey with specks of purple and black.

Grace pulled her collar over her ears as a gust of left-over winter wind whipped up and stung Grace's face. "For Christ sakes, make up your mind. Either be cold or hot. This unpredictability is driving me nuts," Grace mumbled to herself as she turned the corner and walked right into Sarah Child.

They grabbed at each other to stop themselves from falling. "Don't you ever watch where you're going?" she complained as they steadied themselves.

"Usually I do, but who would've guessed you'd be coming around the corner of my home at the same time?"

"I knocked on your door and when there was no answer I decided to try the front store," she said.

Grace gave her a sideways glance and continued to walk back to her apartment, just as the rain started in monsoon fashion. Sarah kept pace alongside Grace.

"Is this a business call or social?" Grace asked as she climbed the stairs ahead of Sarah.

"A little bit of both," she replied as she stood on the back stoop waiting for Grace to open the door.

Grace opened the wooden door and stood inside the kitchen. She turned to look at Sarah, who'd wrapped her coat around her head to try and shield herself from the rain.

"Aren't you going to invite me in?"

Grace sensed that there was more to her visit than meets the eye. She wanted to let her stand out there in the rain until she was soaked to the bone until she developed pneumonia and would have to go to the hospital and have an IV stuck in her arm.

Grace knew Sarah hated needles, and the thought of that would freak her out more than the séance that drove her from her house all those years ago.

Unfortunately, Grace's curiosity got the better of her, and against her better judgment, moved aside to allow Sarah access to her home.

"So what do I owe the pleasure of this visit?" Grace asked sarcastically as she took Sarah's coat and handed her a towel to dry off her hair.

"I can tell by your voice that you're still harbouring some anger towards me," she sighed.

"I'm so over the past," Grace said. It was a lie but Sarah didn't need to know that. "I'd call it more like being cautious."

Sarah put up her hands. "Search me. You'll see that I don't have any rocks with me." She smiled, trying to lighten the already tense mood.

Grace was considering the offer but had second thoughts when she noticed the gun that was exposed under her suit jacket.

"I'll take your word for it," Grace replied. "You're an adult now, so I'm sure rock throwing is behind you. Now you can shoot the person."

Sarah put her arms down and buttoned her jacket. "It's my job. I'm a cop."

"Yeah, I know," Grace replied.

Grace poured some milk into a pot and placed it on the stove. "So you must know Charles." Grace asked already knowing the answer to her question.

Sarah took a seat at the kitchen table. "Sure do. He's my partner."

She knew that, too, but didn't let on.

Grace felt a knot form in her stomach, and she became lightheaded.

Grace turned back to the pot of milk, took a couple of deep breaths and remained silent as the milk foamed and began to boil. "Hot chocolate?"

"Don't mind if I do. Do you have marshmallows?"

Grace pointed to the cupboard above the fridge, and Sarah immediately retrieved a bag of multi-colored miniature marshmallows. She popped some into a couple of mugs, and Grace filled each cup with hot milk and powdered chocolate mixture.

The two women carried their mugs into the living room and got comfortable on the large sofa.

"So you must know Charles pretty good," Grace asked in between sips of her drink.

Sarah shrugged. "Not as good as I want to know him," she replied.

Sarah waited for a response from Grace.

Grace narrowed her eyes at Sarah as she blew on her cocoa and took little sips. She knew what Sarah was fishing for but Grace wasn't about to give her the information Sarah wanted.

"You never told me why you're here," Grace said, nonchalantly.

"Isn't it obvious? "We have a serial killer on the loose, and I'm looking at all possibilities."

"You think I have something to do with the killings?"

Sarah gave out a laugh. "Of course not! I came here for your help."

Grace gave out a half sigh and half moan. "I don't know how I can help you."

"Cut the crap, Grace. Have you any idea how difficult it is for me to be here? How about making it easy for me and conjuring up something from the spirit world to help me catch this bastard before he kills again?"

Grace leaned back and tucked her feet underneath her. "I'd really like to help, Sarah, but nothing I can say or do will help you."

"How can you be so sure?"

"For one thing, you need to believe in my abilities to take anything I say serious. And for another, I'm not going to allow you to come here demanding my help after the way you treated me all these years."

Sarah nodded. "Maybe you're not so over the past as you claim."

"Can you blame me? I mean, you never once gave me the time of day when you saw me on the street. How am I supposed to react? I never did anything wrong to you."

Sarah placed her mug on the table and turned to face Grace. "I'm truly sorry Grace. When I'd see you on the street, I didn't talk to you because I didn't like you. I didn't talk to you because I was embarrassed and ashamed of what I did to you and how I treated you."

"If this is the case, then what's changed? Why are you here now?"

"Because of Charles," she replied without hesitation. "The day after he met you, he came to me and thanked me for the advice I gave him."

"What advice?"

"Now I don't want you to take it the wrong way. I didn't believe that he'd take my suggestion seriously."

"Let me guess. The suggestion of having a psychic on the case was mentioned by you, and Charles took you seriously."

"If you want to put it that way, then yes. It started out as a joke. I told Charles about you and your family and about the setup you had going here on Lundy's Lane. Who would have thought that he'd actually come here to look for help?" She laughed.

"Yeah, who would have thought that?"

"Anyway, he came to me the day after meeting you and thanked me for the advice," she said.

So you decided to come here and size up the competition." Grace grinned.

Sarah shook her head. "There's no competition. If I wanted him, I could have had him a long time ago."

"So how long have you been his partner?" Grace smiled.

Grace knew Sarah was lying. She wanted him, but either she wasn't his type or he didn't allow himself to get involved with anyone at work. Grace chose not to challenge her denial.

"The truth is, I came here to find out how serious you and Charles are. He's, after all, my friend as well as my partner, and I wouldn't want to see him hurt."

"I see. So your visit is out of concern for Charles."

"Exactly!" she replied, pointing her finger in the air.

Grace gathered the empty mugs and took them into the kitchen. Sarah followed closely.

"So are you going to tell me how serious the two of you are?" she asked.

Grace took Sarah's coat from the hook and handed it to her, then opened the wooden door and held it in place. Sarah put on her coat and walked to the door. "I guess that means that it's none of my business."

"Wow! You're good. You must make your captain proud," Grace said.

"Look, Grace. Maybe this came out the wrong way. I just don't want Charles grasping at straws with information that you give him in regards to the case," she said in one last ditch effort to win Grace over.

"I'll tell you what. We're having a séance tonight for that missing girl's mother. I'd like you to be there to see for yourself if what we do is fake or not."

Sarah made a slight whimpering sound as she recalled the last time she was involved in a séance.

Grace secretly hoped history would repeat itself tonight and she would have the pleasure of watching Sarah run screaming from her house.

She thought for a moment. "Okay. What time should I be here?"

"Come at eight," Grace replied just as Sue walked up the stairs and interrupted the women.

Her appearance briefly startled Sarah until recognition hit them both.

"Arrest any perverts lately?" Sue asked Sarah as she stepped past her.

"Sell to any perverts lately?" Sarah asked without missing a beat.

"Only the best perverts," Sue replied. "By the way, when you see your dad, tell him that the Mexican donkey show he ordered last week came in today. He can swing by anytime to pick it up."

Ooh, that was cold, Grace thought.

Sarah turned on her heels and headed down the stairs. "See you at eight," she yelled back ignoring Sue's remark.

Sue narrowed her eyes at Grace. "What do you mean she'll see you at eight?"

TWELVE

Grace closed the door behind her, and Sue followed her into the living room. "She's coming to the séance tonight," Grace said.

Sue flopped herself down on the sofa and rolled her eyes at her friend. "Didn't she run screaming from your house the last time she was involved in a séance with you?"

"Yep, but she was a kid at the time," Grace said.

"Maybe things haven't changed that much, and she'll still freak out," Sue said.

The two women shared a laugh as they ordered a pizza from Antonio's, Grace gave Sue a full reading while they waited for the delivery.

Her reading seemed hopeful in the romance department, and this gave Sue something to look forward to.

An hour later they washed a few slices of pizza down with a beer and were settling on the sofa when there was a knock on the door.

Before Grace had a chance to answer the door, Charles opened it and stepped inside the kitchen. He stopped in his tracks when he saw Grace wasn't alone.

"Sorry, Grace, I didn't realize you have company."

Grace took his coat and hung it in the closet. "Are you off duty?" Grace asked as she took a beer from the fridge.

"Just off duty," he replied, taking the beer.

Sue waved from the living room. "Come on in handsome. We have pizza."

"Two women after my own heart." He took his place between them and grabbed a slice of pizza. He examined the toppings then flicked off all the green olives.

"I never knew you hated green olives?" Grace asked.

"I don't hate them. I just don't like them on pizza."

"But I like them on pizza," Grace said.

"Who in their right mind would order pizza with green olives and pair it up with pineapple?" he said noticing the pineapple beneath the olives.

"I would." Grace said.

"Are you two having a lovers' quarrel? "Sue asked. "Cause if you are, I'm leaving."

"Are we having a lovers' quarrel?" Charles asked.

"That would all depend on whether we're lovers or not."

Grace bit into her pizza and made a yum sound as she tasted the olives and pineapple together."

"Let's call it a lover's discussion over the difference between proper pizza topping and crap." Charles said flicking off another green olive.

"Suits me just fine." Grace smiled.

"How goes the case of that missing girl? Any leads yet?" Sue asked, making small talk and changing the subject.

Charles chewed and swallowed before answering. "Nothing yet, but I hope there'll be a break in the case soon."

"I've been reading the stories in the newspaper and watching the news. It seems that this guy must be from the area," she said.

"We figured that, too, but we need more to go on than that."

"Have you figured out how he's meeting these women?"

Charles nodded. "We think he might be stalking around the night clubs."

Sue mulled over his words. "In theory that would make sense."

Charles looked over at Sue. "You have another thought on this?"

"Sure do."

Grace and Charles stared at Sue as she continued to eat her pizza.

"Are you going to enlighten us or do we have to beat it out of you?" Charles asked laughingly.

Grace put her hand on Charles shoulder. "I wouldn't suggest that to Sue. She might actually take you up on the offer."

Sue narrowed her eyes at Grace. "I would not! I'm not into beatings. I just like an occasional spanking."

"So anyway," Grace said encouragingly to Sue. Whenever Grace started a sentence with those two words, it was a signal for Sue that she's running amuck again and should get back to the main topic of conversation.

This was something Grace used frequently with her as her mind works faster than her mouth.

"If I'm not mistaken, wasn't this last girl under age?" Sue asked.

Charles nodded. "We think she may have been using a fake I.D."

"She could've used a fake ID, but the clubs on the Hill are pretty keen to all fake ID's, even if the ID was from the U.S.A. In my business you have to know these things. You have no idea how many kids try to pass fake ID's when they come into my store."

"I guess we can eliminate the night clubs," Charles said with frustration in his voice. "Besides, she's travelling with her parents, and according to them, she's been with them every evening."

"Has her photo been shown around the tourist area?" Grace asked. "Maybe someone will remember seeing her with someone."

Charles sighed deeply. "We wanted to do that first thing, but our wonderful mayor was against it. He said it would scare away the tourists, and the city would suffer financially."

"I could show her photo," Grace said. "I know all the shop people on the Hill. They might be more willing to help if it came from someone they knew and trusted."

Charles wrapped his arm around Grace's shoulder and squeezed her tight. "I knew there was a reason why I came to you."

Grace felt that familiar fluttering in her stomach, as her temperature raised a couple of degrees from the waist down.

"I guess this is my cue to exit while the two of you get busy?" Sue said making an excuse to leave the room so they could have a few minutes alone time.

"No need to do that Sue, "Grace said as she pulled herself away from Charles.

"Well in that case I wouldn't mind jumping in there and getting one of those sexy hugs," Sue laughed.

Charles obliged by giving Sue a friendly squeeze.

"There's something I need to ask you," Grace said changing the subject.

"Sounds serious. Go ahead and ask me anything."

"What's your relationship with Sarah?" Grace asked."Apart from her being your partner, is there anything else going on between the two of you?"

He looked puzzled. "She's my partner and my friend," Charles replied. "Why do you ask?"

Grace shrugged. "Your partner paid me a visit today."

Charles stopped in mid bite with his mouth open. "She did? What did she want?"

"To be honest I think she was here to feel out the competition."

"My relationship with Sarah is strictly professional," Charles said in defence.

"I've no doubt about that. But I get the feeling that she is either reading more into your friendship than what's really there or she's hoping for more."

Charles leaned back on the sofa. "Why do I get the feeling there's no love lost between the two of you?"

Grace nodded. "Sarah and I go back a long way. I'm surprised she didn't tell you about our relationship."

"I gather by the tone in your voice it wasn't that great of a relationship."

"On the contrary, it was more like a love, hate relationship."

"Yeah." Sue jumped in. "Sarah loved to throw rocks at Grace and Grace hated every minute of it,"

"I'd never have pegged Sarah as the rock-throwing kind," he said trying to lighten the mood.

"Anyway, she's joining us tonight for the séance," Grace said.

"I never thought she was the séance type person either," Charles said.

"She isn't," Grace muttered under her breath.

Grace helped her mother set the ambience of the room for the séance as the guests arrived on time. Charles and Sue helped light candles as Sarah swung her ass through the front door.

She was dressed down in a pair of tight jeans that were beyond camel toe crotch, a low cut pink sweater that showed her twins up close and personal, and stiletto boots.

"I guess she's out to impress tonight," Sue whispered to Grace.

"Either that or she just got off duty pretending to be a prostitute to lure John's down on Bridge St.

"I thought she did that for recreational purposes." Sue added.

That brought a snicker from both girls.

Love and Murder on the Hill

They watched her strut over to Charles, who was grilling Grace's mother with questions about what to expect during the séance.

"Hi, Charles," she said as she locked her arm in his.

"Sarah, nice that you could join us," mom said.

Sarah made no attempt to make eye contact with her. She kept her gaze on Charles, who was beginning to feel a bit uncomfortable with Sarah's behavior.

"Aren't you going to say hi?" he asked his partner.

Sarah managed a fake smile and mumbled something that sounded similar to hello and kiss my ass, then turned her attention back to Charles.

Grace wanted to smack Sarah upside her head. It was one thing to disrespect Grace, but she drew the line when it came to her family members.

Grace walked over to where Sarah and Charles were and took Sarah by the arm. "You don't mind if I borrow your work partner for a moment?" Grace asked Charles as she led Sarah into the other room.

Grace closed the door behind them. "Sarah, you may not like me for whatever reason, but while you're in my family's home, I expect you to show respect to my mother and grandmother." Grace's voice was stern, and she meant business.

Sarah stepped back slightly. "I thought that's what I was doing," she replied.

Grace gave herself a mental slap on the forehead. "I knew it was a bad mistake inviting you. You'll ruin this evening for Becky's parents."

"It's just a stupid séance. How can anyone ruin that?"

Grace blew out a sigh and silently counted to ten. When ten didn't help her to calm down, she continued to twenty. "You can't participate if you don't have some belief in it. Non believers will make it difficult for us to contact the spirit world."

She threw her hands in the air. "Okay, whatever. I'll try to be on my best behavior so that we can get through this evening and go back to our real lives."

Now that Grace had convinced her to behave during the séance, her next thoughts were on Sarah keeping her paws off of Charles.

But Grace didn't know exactly where she stood with Charles.

Sure, they were intimate in more ways than she'd been with anyone in the past. Sure, he was always calling and coming over. But they'd just met, and it was too soon to call their relationship a commitment. Grace thought it best not to get into a territory cat fight for the moment.

Sarah and Grace rejoined the rest of the group just as Becky's parents arrived. They were pale from worry, and Becky's mother seemed to have lost weight since her first television interview pleading for the safe return of their daughter. Not unusual, given the trauma they were going through.

They recognized Charles and immediately questioned him on the case. He could only give them what he knew, and that summed up to almost zero.

Becky's mother spotted Grace from across the room and touched her husband's arm while pointing in Grace's direction. They both made their way over to where she was.

"It dawned on me after my visit I never introduced myself," she said as she took Grace's hand.

"I'm Sheila Saunders and this is Becky's father, Harold," she said squeezing Grace's hand.

Harold nodded and took Grace's hand without saying a word. It was obvious that he was more distraught over his daughter missing than Sheila was.

"Becky was our world," he whispered. "I don't know." He stopped short of his sentence as the words were caught in his throat. He was a big, towering man, and to see him with so much pain in his eyes made Grace sad. It also made her more determined to find the person responsible for bringing this man to his knees.

"We'll try our best to help you," Grace assured the couple.

"I would like you both to meet my grandmother and mother," Grace said, taking the couple into the dining room.

Mom and granny were busy setting the dining room table with a selection of sandwiches and sweets for afterwards.

"Mom. Granny. I want you to meet Becky's parents, Sheila and Harold Saunders," Grace said.

Grace turned to the Saunders. "This is my mom Celia and my grandmother Mary."

The four people shook hands and Becky's parents thanked the two women for doing this for them.

"You understand that if we do have contact with your daughter that it may mean she is no longer with the living." Mary said.

Love and Murder on the Hill

The couple lowered their heads. "We just need to know if this is the case, then we hope she's at peace."

Grace came into the library and motioned to everyone they were ready to begin.

She directed the guests to their assigned seats putting Grace between the Saunders and her mother next to Harold and her grandmother next to Sheila.

Charles sat between Sue and Celia while Sarah was positioned between Sue and Granny. This helped create a strong line of communication between Grace and Becky's parents without any weakness in the circle.

Candles lit the table as Grace's grandmother asked everyone to hold hands and pray. This was a normal ritual when beginning a séance.

"We asked God to watch over us during this time," granny prayed. "We ask our spirit guides to bring forth the people we call," mom said.

The prayers helped relax everyone, but in reality it was to ask God for protection from any hostile spirits that may try to contact the group. This was something they didn't want the guest to know.

No need to panic them with the possibility of mean spirits rising up to wreak havoc.

They continued by asking God to help any spirits that roamed the earth, he would find them and bring them home.

After they all said amen, the séance began.

It took several minutes for the first contact. Henry, Grace's slave spirit, was the first contact to make an appearance. During this time he tried to make contact with Becky. Grace spoke to Henry as she was the only one who heard him. He tried for several more minutes but couldn't contact Becky.

"Is this a good sign?" Sheila asked.

Grace nodded. "If he was able to contact her then this would mean her spirit isn't in our realm. She's either still alive or has moved on to the world beyond Henry's."

Grace watched as Harold blinked tears from his eyes.

Granny called for her spirit to enter the circle. The candles flickered as Elizabeth joined the group.

Elizabeth had been granny's spirit since she developed her skills as a child.

Elizabeth was a young girl from medieval times. Her father sold her to royalty as a lady in waiting, but soon caught the attention of the king. He pursued her even though she wasn't older than fifteen. One night she fled the castle and made her way back home. Her father was outraged at her selfishness when she showed up at his doorstep.

He was given certain privileges because his daughter was given the position of a lady in waiting. All this would be taken away from him if they discovered Elizabeth missing. She told her father of the king's plans for her and how he would come to visit her while she slept, but this just fueled anger toward her.

The thought of becoming a mistress of the king was even more a privilege than being a lady in waiting. He took the girl back to the castle, but before he did so he beat her unconscious.

Once back at the castle, he offered his daughter to the king for his pleasure and left his injured daughter to be raped and abused by him.

After several months, she became pregnant. The last thing she wanted was to have a child by the man she grew to hate, so one day she threw herself off the highest tower of the castle. Because she had committed suicide, she was destined to roam between both worlds until someone helped her cross over.

Mary had planned to take her to the other side when she, too, passed on.

This promise kept Elizabeth with her all these years, and they developed a slightly unorthodox friendship.

Grace listened as her grandmother talked to Elizabeth as if it were two old friends meeting after a long absence. She asked the spirit about Becky. A few more words were exchanged, then there was silence.

Grace felt Becky's spirit enter her body.

She was to be the path of communication between both worlds.

Sheila and Harold gasped as their daughter's spirit quickly apologized for leaving. At first they accepted what was going on' then they became skeptical.

"How do we know you're Becky?" Harold asked.

"Ask me anything that no one here would know," Becky said through Grace.

Harold thought for a moment. "On your sixteenth birthday I gave you a daughter's ring. Inside the ring I engraved something for you. What did it say?" he asked.

Without hesitation Grace answered his question. "My life is complete. Love daddy."

Becky's parents broke down crying.

"Don't cry, mommy and daddy. I'm okay. Grandma is with me, and she sends her love."

"Who did this to you?" Charles asked.

Becky went silent.

Grace's mother repeated Charles' question.

Becky became agitated. "Joe did this. He pretended to like me, but he isn't who he says he is."

"Do you know where he lives?" Mom asked.

"I see lots of trees. Like the country." Becky went silent again.

"Are you still with us, Becky?" mom asked.

"It's cold and wet where I am. I shouldn't have gone with Joe. I want to go back with grandma. She wants to take me home," Becky said. "Can I go now?"

"Yes, Becky. You can go now," Mom said.

"Don't cry, mommy and daddy. We'll see each other again. I'm happy now."

Her last words before she left Grace were her love for her parents.

Grace slumped back in her chair, and Sue asked if she was alright.

When someone's body is taken over by a spirit, it can be physically as well as mentally draining. Granny poured Grace a glass of water. Grace took it with her trembling hands and sipped slowly.

Sarah sat silently, not taking her eyes off of Grace.

"What's wrong?" Grace asked her between sips.

"How did you do that?" she asked.

"Do what?"

She shook her head in disbelief. "How did the room go from warm to ice cold when you said you were Becky?"

"Still don't believe?" Grace asked Sarah.

She stood and quickly left the room without answering.

"You can't teach an old dog new tricks," Sue whispered to Grace.

"And you can't put them down either." Grace added.

"That was unbelievable!" Charles said, moving closer.

"Thanks, I think," Grace replied.

"I've never been to a séance before, and this just blew my mind. It was so cool. Can we do it again sometime?" He sounded like a child who just rode a rollercoaster for the very first time in his life.

"Okay. But next time someone else can be the contact," Grace said.

He kissed Grace on the cheek just as Sarah walked back into the room. She stopped in her tracks at the sight of her partner kissing her arch enemy, then turned on her stilettos and made a hasty retreat.

"I think you need to eat something," Mom said handing Grace a plate of sandwiches.

Grace wolfed one down and felt her strength coming back.

"Let's join everyone in the dining room," Grace said to Sue and Charles.

They grabbed a plate and filled them with goodies as mom and granny talked in their comforting voices to Becky's parents.

"I can't believe this has happened to our daughter," Harold sobbed. "My little girl is gone."

His wife sat in silence, mulling over all that had happened. Her face showed disbelief at the loss of her daughter.

Grace watched as granny sat beside Sheila, putting her arm around her, trying her best to comfort the woman. She didn't shed a tear or say a word. She just sat, staring into space.

"Is Becky really gone?" Charles whispered to Grace.

Grace nodded.

"I feel so bad for her parents," he said.

"Me, too."

Sheila's attention turned to Charles. She stood and walked over to where he was standing. "You need to find my daughter's body so we can bring her home."

Charles nodded. "We'll do everything we can to find her."

Sheila nodded a thank you and walked over to her husband who was slumped in a chair with his face in his hands. She put her hand on his shoulder and he looked up at his wife.

"Time to go," she said.

Harold followed Sheila out the front door and they disappeared into the night.

Silence filled the room as they watched the couple leave quietly.

"Where's Sarah?" Sue asked, looking around the room.

"She left in a hurry," granny replied. "And she wasn't too pleased when she left."

"Why do you say that?" Grace asked.

"She said a few choice words which I don't care to repeat, before she went out the back and slammed the door behind her."

It was past midnight when the last of the visitors said their goodbyes. Granny had retired over an hour ago and Sue left shortly after. Charles and Grace stayed behind to help her mom wrap up the rest of the sandwiches.

Mom handed a plate of goodies to Charles and insisted he take them home. He obliged and placed the plate next to his jacket.

Grace stretched her arms and gave out a yawn. "I should be going too. I want to set up my table for tomorrow morning."

Charles stood and helped Grace on with her coat. "Let me walk you home," he whispered.

Celia smiled as she let them out the back door. "Sleep tight you two," she said as if she knew something they didn't know.

THIRTEEN

Joe sat on his sofa staring at the television. The news was reporting on the weather as he waited for any news on whether Becky was found. It had been three days since he dropped her body in the Niagara River. His hope of having them find the body were beginning to fade.

"These cops are so bloody slow in doing their jobs," he muttered to himself. "Her body should be at the bottom of the falls by now."

The news was almost over, and there's still nothing on his latest victim. He checked his watch, flicked off the TV and headed out the front door. He was angry that it was taking them so long to find the body. He needed their attention on something else so he could make his move for his next victim.

He climbed in his car and revved the engine. Grey smoke sputtered out the exhaust as Joe put it in reverse and backed out his long driveway. "I can't wait for those village idiots to find the girl. I need to have another fix now," he said to himself as he backed onto the road, popped the car in drive, and headed toward, the falls.

The weather was warm and sunny and sure to bring out new young blood in skimpy tees and shorts. Joe was a looker and had no problem drawing the attention of some young girls who were begging for it. But he always played it cool.

He didn't want to set his sights on just anyone. He needed one who was alone, cute enough to satisfy his desires, but plain enough to not have other guys falling over themselves to get her attention. She needed to be invisible to everyone but him.

It was much easier to find someone when there's a lot of people on the Hill as opposed to just a few tourists. Everyone would be too busy with the sights to notice him talking to his next victim. Everyone would be too busy looking at the pretty girls to notice a girl who was just a step up from plain.

The afternoon sun warmed up the last bit of winter chill and brought out the remainder of hibernators from their homes. The sky was crystal blue with just a few specks of white.

Grace was too deeply involved in the reading of a tourist to notice Charles watching her from the distance. He leaned against the building crossing his arms and smiling as he watched the new love of his life doing her job.

It was hard to believe that he'd seen her many times, but never paid notice until he saw her standing in her mother's house with a towel wrapped around her head. Who would have known that when they met that day, his thoughts would be filled with only her? Which left a permanent smile on his face and warmth in his heart at the mere mention of her name?

Since the day they met he'd drive up Clifton Hill to get a glimpse of her in action. Sometimes he would park his car and just observe her from a distance, just as he's doing now.

He never approached her. He didn't want to disturb her during work or let her think he's a freak who stalked women. He just wanted to see her in her natural zone as a fortune teller. Charles wanted to have his daily Grace fix.

After his first intimate moment with Grace, he wanted to take her home to meet his parents. He wanted to share everything with the woman he had known for less than a month, but he knew it was too soon for that. He didn't want to rush Grace into a commitment.

With her, he had to take small steps to not frighten her away. He knew so much about her, yet so little. One thing he did know for sure, she was alienated as a child because of her family. If only the tormentors would have taken the time to know the family.

They are wonderful people and never pass judgment on anyone. Celia and Mary reminded him of his own parents. He hadn't seen his family for a few months. He was so busy with his work and the move to Niagara Falls, Charles didn't have time to visit with them.

They talked on the phone everyday when he moved, but that was the extent of their contact. Now that there was this possible serial killer on the loose, his calls were cut down to three times a week and consisted of a few minutes of greetings and miss you before he'd get back to whatever he was working on at the time.

Now he was spending every free moment with Grace and loved every second of their time together. But he was still unsure how she was feeling about him. She rarely called him. He was doing all the pursuing, which was a new experience for him.

In the past, the women he'd been involved with would constantly make their feelings known with calls and unscheduled visits. But here he was, standing in the shadows watching the woman who'd made his heart skip a beat with just a smile and wanting nothing more than to spend every moment with her.

I guess this must be love, he thought as he put his hands in his pockets.

His thoughts of love and lust were interrupted by the sound of his cell phone.

"We found a woman's body," Sarah said to her partner.

"Where are you?" he asked, his voice serious.

After a quick briefing of the location, he hung up, turned on his heels, and hurried to his car.

Ten minutes later he was standing on the shore of the Niagara river, about a half mile up from the Falls. Sarah joined her partner as they watched the rescue boat retrieve the body which was snagged on some rocks.

"Who spotted the body?" Charles asked.

"A couple of guys were out fishing and noticed something over by the rocks," She said, pointing to two young men standing by the shore watching the scene. "It wasn't until they got a little closer they realized it was a body."

Charles looked over at the two men who were obviously shaken by their find.

"Anyone spoke to them yet?" he asked.

"A couple of uniforms were taking notes. I was waiting till you got here to approach them," she said.

"Wait till they bring the body to shore while I go over and have a few words with them." He excused himself and made his way over to the men.

The three of them stood watching as the body was lifted into the boat. The men gasped at the sight, lowered their heads, and breathed deeply.

"It must have been a shock to see that," Charles said as his eyes stayed fixed on the rescue boat.

They both nodded in silence.

"You both realize that you risked your lives to get your boat that close to the rapids?"

The two men couldn't have been much older than twenty five.

They're dressed in cut offs and tee shirts advertising a past Blue Rodeo concert in Niagara Falls. Charles knew if he searched their boat he'd be sure to find beer on board.

"What were you doing out so far near the rapids? You know that area is off limits to boaters," Charles said.

"We know but we were curious to see what it was," the smaller man said. "Are we going to get in trouble for this? Cause if we are my dad's gonna kill me."

"Not unless you had something to do with this, then no," Charles replied.

"Can we go now?" the other young man asked.

Charles nodded. "Give one of the officers your information in case we need to contact you later."

They hurried away from the edge of the water toward a uniformed officer who was busy cordoning off the area with yellow caution tape.

Charles jogged back to his partner's side.

"Who's going to inform Becky's parents?" Sarah asked.

Charles shrugged. "I haven't the heart to tell them,"

Sarah blew out a sigh. "Okay, fine, I'll tell them, but you owe me one."

She turned and headed to her car, her long red hair bouncing with each step she took.

Charles watched Sarah's car pulled out of the parking lot and disappear down the parkway.

The area where the body was found consisted mostly of park area for locals to picnic in. Houses lined the other side of the road but were situated far back from the main road to allow for more privacy.

Charles walked through the park along the rivers edge, looking for any sign of where the body could have been disposed of. A fence was erected along the shore to protect people from accidently falling in. Doesn't look like an area that would be easy to drop off a body, Charles thought.

He took his cell from his pocket and punched in Grace's number.

A smile formed on his face as he heard Grace's voice. "Feel like taking a break?"

Grace handed Charles a mug of hot chocolate and took her place across from him. He seemed down, and she had a sneaky suspicion she knew what it was. "You found Becky," Grace said above a whisper.

He took a sip from his cup and nodded sadly.

Grace reached out and touched his arm to let him know she was there for him. "I'm so sorry, Charles. I wish I could say something to make things better, but I know there's no words that can do this."

"It's okay, Grace. Just being here for me is worth more than anything."

A tear trickled down Grace's cheek, and she quickly wiped it away before Charles could see how his mood affected her. They hadn't known each other long, yet at this moment Grace felt as if they'd known each other all their lives. At this very moment Grace felt closer to him than she had ever felt with anyone. As much as Grace didn't want to admit it, she was quickly falling in love with this man.

Warm summer-like weather welcomed in the month of June and Grace was busy reading fortunes in her regular spot. It had been almost three weeks since Becky's body was found, and summer was officially in full swing. Her parents accompanied their daughter's body back to their home, but kept in touch with the local police on any break in the case.

Nothing new had developed. The police were at the same dead end as when the first body was recovered. The only new information they had was the first body wasn't a random act of violence.

They were dealing with a serial killer, and this person needed to be stopped before another report of a missing person crossed their desk.

Serial Killer Loose in Niagara Falls, was headline news on the front page of every newspaper within a two hundred mile radius. The television news stations as well as the radio stations blamed the police for not warning the public sooner about this killer on the loose.

The mayor was being called to the plate on why nothing was being done and in turn he put the pressure on Sarah and Charles who were heading the investigation.

In spite of the pressure Charles was under, his relationship with Grace was heating up just like the weather. Grace, on the other hand, was worried about the relationship as well as the killer.

As much as Grace had developed deep feelings for him, she was afraid that it would end up at a dead end, like so many of her other relationships.

He was already comfortable with Grace's family and he loved them for themselves. This made their relationship easier to manage. But Grace was a realist, and she knew that, for their relationship to develop deeper, she'd have to win the approval of his family.

They talked about it on a few occasions, but it never went further than that. No commitment to meeting them was ever made or she'd find a way to change the subject. Grace was afraid his family might not approve of her.

"You look deep in thought," a familiar voice said.

Grace looked up to see her mother smiling down at her.

"Was just thinking," Grace said.

She slipped into the empty seat across from her daughter. "I can see that. Anything I can help you with?"

Grace shook her head. "I was thinking about Charles and his family."

"I wouldn't worry about them. I'm sure they'll love you," she assured her daughter, taking her hand and patting it gently.

Her words were comforting, but deep down Grace wasn't so worried about them liking her as much as she worried about them accepting her family.

Grace had a lot of growing to do, and she needed to stop worrying about people talking about her mother and grandmother in a negative way.

After all, it was the twenty-first century, and things had changed since Grace was a little girl.

People were more understanding and accepting of other's beliefs and practices. Maybe this would be the case with Charles' family.

Grace shook her body to rid herself of any negative thoughts. Think positive and stop worrying so much about things that haven't happened. Grace thought.

FOURTEEN

Joe took his place on one of the many benches that lined the street of Clifton Hill. He removed his hamburger and fries from the fast food bag, took a bite of his burger and washed it down with a large sip of Coke.

The mid-day sun brought out the people in droves, and by noon Clifton Hill was a bustling crowd of tourists and locals alike.

He always sat on the same bench at the same time of day. He'd done so since working on the Hill. Some faces were familiar, such as the locals who worked the area, but during the summer there were new faces of tourists who drove over the border to see the sights.

Since the casinos were established, Joe saw Clifton Hill go from almost a ghost-like street to wall to wall people. The shops and local sights upgraded to top quality, and even a few new places laid down roots on the main drag.

But Joe was a local and worked the area well. His business thrived, and he was able to hire a couple of students during the weekends and summer months. This gave him more time to pursue his passion and dreams. For the past few years Joe only dreamed of doing the unthinkable.

When he was younger, he started out peeking into windows to watch women, but this wasn't satisfying enough. This also proved a bit risky since he was known in the area.

Getting caught by the cops would've been a death sentence to his obsession as well as an embarrassment to his mother. So he abandoned his peeping tom ways and opted for sitting on the bench and people-watching all the while fantasizing of ways to fulfill his urges.

He'd read a story about women being spied on through peep holes in public washrooms or motel rooms, but this too wasn't something he wanted to dabble in. Not only would it be nearly impossible to achieve, but if he was ever caught, he could only imagine what would happen to him.

So he was back to square one.

Every day he'd sit, watch, and dream. Occasionally while working he'd see a woman or young girl who would catch his eye, and sometimes he'd catch her eye.

He'd arrange a date for that evening and hope to see where the date would get him. But most weren't as accepting of his sexual fantasies. Some would go as far as to call him a perverted pig.

He hated to be judged, especially by some slut who played games with him. So once again he was back to the beginning. But his urges got the better of him, and to his luck, his mother passed away and left him the family home. It was a nice house in a nice area of town, but too open for prying eyes.

During one of his drives along the parkway he came upon a small cottage that sat hidden from the road. It was in dire need of work, but it sat secluded on five acres of wooded area. It was the perfect place for Joe to make his fantasies become reality. The sale of the family home gave him enough cash to buy the place and fix it up so he could put his plan into action.

Once he had the place, he had to find the right girl. But he had to be careful. She could never be traced back to him. He'd already made one mistake with the first girl. He knew her. They had history, but she'd never been reported missing. At least not yet.

Her family lived across the country, and they were estranged from each other. Even so, the link between Jen and himself could destroy him.

The only thing he had going for him was her body hadn't been found, and he was a good liar. He'd already concocted his story in case the cops ever came knocking. It helped to know someone who was part of the investigation.

Being a childhood friend of Sarah's made it easier. She always thought he was a great guy. He was always polite to her and never got into trouble with the law. They even dated for a brief time, but still remained friends until he went off to college and she went off to the police academy.

Love and Murder on the Hill

They were still friends as far as he was concerned, even though they lost touch. He'd seen her a few times out and about on Clifton Hill walking the beat when she was in uniform.

He never approached her to pick up where they left off. He didn't want to be too obvious. She eventually made detective, and his sightings of her were few and far between. He did manage to run into her mother one day while he was working.

As usual, she couldn't resist boasting how Sarah became detective and was part of the homicide team investigating the murders. He pretended to be uninterested, yet secretly he hung on her every word.

Joe reached into his back pocket and pulled out his wallet. He rummaged through it and removed a piece of paper with Sarah's cell number. Maybe I should call her and inch back into her life? He thought as he stared at the number her mother scribbled on the paper.

He finished his hamburger, wiped his mouth, and punched in Sarah's number on his cell.

"It's great to hear from you. My mother told me she ran into you the other day," Sarah said.

After an exchange of words and some catching up, they made a date for Saturday.

Joe popped the rest of his fries in his mouth, dumped the trash in the nearest bin and headed back to his job. A smile formed on his face as he thought how smart he was. Having an inside contact with the cops will prove beneficial to his secret work, he thought. Beneficial indeed.

Joe rounded the corner and caught a glimpse of Grace sitting at her table selling her trade. He stood at the corner out of sight all the while watching her intently.

He had always had a thing for her while growing up, but she was the misfit, and his buddies would've given him a ribbing if he ever went out with her. But he was older now and much more mature.

He thought of approaching her, but he wasn't so nice to her growing up. His fantasies of her were even less nice. He doubted if she would easily forgive and forget his childhood tormenting. "In time," he said to himself. "I'll have you in time."

Grace looked up from her reading as she felt a cold chill on the back of her neck. She quickly glanced around to see where it was coming from, but there were too many people in the walkway to see the source of the chill. Someone was watching her, and that persons thoughts were disturbing. Grace shook it off and turned her concentration back to the customer's palm.

"I see an upcoming proposal of some type," Grace said. "It isn't a marriage proposal but some type of job proposal. You're either changing your job for a better one or you're going to get a better position in the company you're in now. Either way, you should take it. It'll be the best move for you."

The young girl squealed with delight. "That's fantastic! I'm hoping I'll get this new position!"

Grace let go of her hand and told her that was all she could see.

The girl paid Grace for her reading. "You're fantastic! I wish you lived in my city. You would make millions doing this for all my friends."

Grace smiled and stuffed the money in her fanny pack.

"Why don't you stop by our store on the way out of town? I have a website that you can check out as well." Grace handed her one of the brochures, and she took it without hesitation.

"I will certainly do that." She thanked Grace once more, then disappeared into the crowd.

It was near dusk when Grace decided to call it a night. Aaron and Marco were already packing up to leave as Grace gathered her belongings and made the short trek to her car. "Want some help with that?" a voice asked.

Grace jumped, and her heart skipped a beat as she whirled around and found Marco standing inches from her.

"Thanks, but I got it."

He ignored Grace's words, shoved her umbrella in the trunk, and slammed the door shut. "There, that should do it."

Grace unlocked her car door and had it open by the time he realized she wasn't beside him.

"Want to go for a coffee?" he asked as he moved toward Grace.

Grace quickly slid into the car, closed the door, and gunned the engine. "Thanks, but no thanks," she said through the closed window.

Marco stood there with slight frustration by Grace's response. "Come on. Just one coffee. I promise to keep my hands above the table."

Love and Murder on the Hill

Grace rolled her window down. "It's not your hands that concern me."

Marco gave out a laugh. "Okay, I promise no rocks in my pockets either."

His joke managed to get a smile out of Grace. She sat for a moment and gave it some thought. "If I agree will you promise to stop hounding me?"

"Scouts honor," Marco said holding up two fingers.

That remark might have worked on someone else, but Grace knew Marco. He was never in the scouts or cubs for that matter."

"Okay, but just one coffee, and you take your own car just in case."

He smiled showing his white veneers and hurried to his car.

Five minutes later they were sitting at an outdoor coffee house sipping on a couple of lattes.

"See? Hands on the table." He smiled.

Grace ignored him and sipped her drink in silence.

"Are you going to see your new boyfriend later?" he asked breaking the silence.

"Who are you talking about?"

He took a sip of his latte. "That good looking cop. You know, Sarah Child's partner."

Grace always knew that in spite of the surge of tourists in Niagara Falls, it was really a small town. If someone coughed, everyone covered their mouths. This was another prime example of why Grace had desperately wanted to leave for a bigger city where no one knew her and didn't care what she did for a living.

"How do you know about him?"

Marco leaned back in his chair and grinned. "I have my ways."

"I bet your ways have something to do with Sarah and her big mouth."

He shook his head and sipped his latte. "Nope. Her mother's mouth is bigger. Ran into her the other day and she told me."

Grace gave out a sound that was a cross between a laugh and a snort. "Yeah, I forgot about that busy body. She was the first to condemn my family to hell, yet she was a regular customer of my grandmother's."

"I never took her for that type of customer," he said.

"You'd be surprised which type she is and the stores she would venture into."

"You're not saying." He cut himself off.

Grace just smiled and sipped her drink.

"I guess you heard about this nutcase going around kidnapping women and killing them," Marco asked.

Grace nodded. "Yeah. So far they have four bodies but I think there's another one."

"Really? Why do you think that?" Marco asking moving closer.

Grace pointed to an imaginary line that Marco crossed and he moved back to his original spot. "I just have a feeling there's another one out there that no one's found yet."

Marco shook his body. "It freaks me out that some dude is out there doing this in our city. If I ever caught the S.O.B. I'd castrate his nuts and hang him out to dry."

The corners of Grace's mouth curled slightly at the thought of Marco doing this to anyone. "You think you could do that?"

Marco nodded. "You betcha. I would beat the shit out of the sucker."

"I find that quite interesting because I remember a time in biology class when we had to cut a worm in two and you fainted before you even got your worm out of the box," Grace laughed.

"Well I told the teacher I didn't like worms. It had nothing to do with cutting the thing. I just don't like worms," Marco said in his defense.

"Sure, sure Marco." Grace laughed.

Their conversation turned serious. "Can you think of anyone who might be capable of doing these things?" Grace asked.

Marco thought for a moment. "A few people come to mind."

"Like who?"

"Old man Hopper who owns the wax museum for one," Marco said. "You know when you walk over by the wax guard air blows up from the floor?"

"Yeah, I remember getting that gust a wind up my butt a couple of times."

Do you know he has a hidden camera on the floor there too?"

Grace shook her head. "He does? What the hell for?"

"Old man Hopper sits behind the ticket counter and waits for some nice looking woman in a skirt. Once they're standing over top of the camera, he shoots the air just enough to lift the skirt a little. When the air blows the camera snaps a photo of what's underneath." Marco gave out a laugh.

Grace gasped. Her mother and grandmother had been hit with that blast of wind as well as herself. The thought of that dirty old man wanking to photos of her family's panties disgusted her.

"How'd you know this?" Grace asked suspiciously.

"Saw some of the photos when I was working there one summer. The old man has a room that he keeps locked for his own enjoyment. He forgot to lock it one day and I happened to walk in and saw everything."

"Jesus H Christ," Grace gasped. "I knew there was something weird about him but I just chalked it up to him hanging around wax figures all day." Grace took a deep breath to stop her drink and any leftover lunch reappearing.

"I doubt if he has anything to do with the killings though," Marco said. "He may be a pervert but he's a harmless one."

"For once I have to agree with you on that," Grace said. "The guy we're looking for is someone who's young and good looking. Someone the girls can feel comfortable with."

"Like me." Marco laughed.

Exactly. Someone just like you."

"I said, like me. Doesn't mean I'm involved in this," Marco said defensively. "I love women too much to want to hurt them."

Marco ordered two more lattes as they sat quietly, thinking about who would be a possible candidate for murder.

"How can we be sure it's someone local?" he asked.

"We can't be sure, but given the fact that some were tourists and their bodies are washing up on the Niagara River, evidence points to a local," Grace replied.

"My guess is that this person works the Hill and that's how he's meeting these women."

Marco nodded in agreement.

"What about the Haunted Mansion?" Marco suggested. "Lots of young freaks working there."

Grace shook her head. "Those freaks are the Summers boys. They always look like that except for the costumes. They spend their time dressed as creatures running around scaring people. Pretty difficult to pick up girls doing that sort of thing."

"Yep. Point taken on that one," Marco laughed.

"And besides, neither one have a car." She added.

"Question," Marco asked after a moment of thought. "Is it true you did it with Jeremy Summers?"

Grace rolled her eyes. "For the love of God and all that's holy. I never did it with Jeremy."

"Just asking cause he told everyone you and he did it in his backyard pup tent."

"Let me set the record straight on what happened in his pup tent. We were playing cards and he asked if he could touch my breasts."

"Did you let him?" Marco asked.

"Yes I let him. I didn't see any harm in it."

"I bet you didn't until he got to school and told everyone that you and he did it." Marco laughed.

"It goes to show you who your friends really were in school." Grace sighed.

Marco shivered. "Yeah but Jeremy? The guy has red eyes. The whole nest of them have red eyes. That's way too freaky even for me, and I've seen some freaky shit."

Grace did another eye roll. "They don't have red eyes. Their eyes are blue and blood shot most of the time from working in the dark. Besides Jeremy was my friend and I thought he was cute."

Grace thought for a moment. "Then again, I thought the Back Street Boys were cute too."

"You could've had anyone. Even I thought you were kinda sexy back then," Marco said.

"If you thought that way then why were you and your friends always tormenting the crap out of me?"

Marco reached over and messed Grace's hair. "You dummy, that's how guys showed girls they like them. All my buddies had the hots for you and we felt that way even before the Jeremy scandal."

Grace shrugged. "What did I know back then? I was fifteen and my hormones were all over the place."

"So now that you know I thought you were hot, would you ever consider going out with me?" Marco asked.

"Not on your life," Grace replied.

Marco gave out a deep sigh of disappointment and the two of them went back to people staring.

FIFTEEN

Grace checked her watch as she finished her latte. It was past seven and she felt her stomach rumble. "I better get going," she said. "I need to get some food in me."

"I can buy you supper." He said with hope in his voice.

"Thanks but no thanks,"

Marco sat back in his chair, arms crossed. "You still don't trust me?"

"It's not that. It's just that I think I'm in a relationship with a cop."

"So you're not quite sure? How the hell can you not be sure?" Marco asked.

"Well, I'm pretty sure I am."

"Okay, okay. If you find out for sure whether you are or not and it turns out that you aren't would you have dinner with me sometime?"

Grace felt as if the whole coffee thing went a full circle but she was beginning to see that Marco wasn't such a bad ass after all." I might consider it."

Marco raised his hands. "There is a God after all," he shouted to no one in particular.

"I said might." Grace reminded him as she took out her keys.

They parted ways, and a few minutes later Grace was channel surfing in her living room. Her mother invited Grace for supper, which she eagerly accepted, and took the liberty to ask Charles if he wanted to join them. His voice seemed preoccupied, but did accept the invite and would be over in an hour.

"An hour to myself," Grace murmured as she sunk her tired body deeper into the soft sofa.

Grace felt herself drift as the soothing sounds of the television put her to sleep. Grace went into a deep R.E.M state and found herself dreaming of her childhood.

She dreamt of being surrounded by Marco, Aaron, and Sarah. They were laughing and pushing her, all the while calling Grace the witch of Niagara. Grace was angry, yet scared at the same time. Then Jeremy appeared and started tugging on Grace's shirt all the while asking to see her boobies.

Grace felt herself being pulled from the dream into the waking evening by the sound of someone at her door.

She dragged her sleepy body from the sofa and went to the kitchen to see Charles standing on her porch waving.

"I was knocking for ten minutes. I thought something happened to you," he said as he kissed Grace on the cheek.

She stretched her arms and gave out a yawn. "Sorry. I fell asleep on the couch and was deep in dreamland. Didn't hear you."

He took a soda from the fridge. "Maybe I should have my own key just in case."

Grace blinked twice and her eyes widened. "Just in case of what?"

Charles popped the tab open and chugged his drink. "Just in case you're sleeping or taking a shower. That way, I can let myself in."

His face showed hope, but Grace felt stomach pains at his suggestion.

She'd never given anyone a key to her apartment except her family.

She valued her privacy, and although she was developing deep feelings for Charles, she believed it was too soon to allow him a spot in her bathroom for his toothbrush and razor.

"Or maybe not." His smile disappeared, and his eyes spoke of hurt feelings.

"It's not that I wouldn't love to have you here all the time; it's just that we haven't known each other that long, and I'm still not sure how far this relationship will go."

Charles nodded in agreement. He reached into his pocket, pulled out a key, and handed it to Grace. "I thought you'd say that, but until you're ready to take our relationship further, I want you to have this."

Grace looked at the key with curiosity. "What's this for?"

He finished his drink and tossed the empty can into the recycling bin. "It's a key to my place. I want you to feel as if my place is your place."

Grace was confused. She hadn't even thought about sharing their private space with each other, yet he was willing to do so in the short time they'd been seeing each other.

"There's only one thing wrong with this," Grace said.

"What would that be?"

"I've never seen your apartment or know where you live."

"Hmm. You're right." He shrugged. "Well, there's only one solution to that. You need to pack an overnight bag and come home with me tonight."

"Let's worry about that later," Grace said as she looked at her watch and realized they were late for supper.

Grace was quiet throughout supper, and her mother sensed something wasn't quite right. When the moment allowed itself, she inquired about her daughter's silence.

"I have a lot on my mind," Grace said.

"Let's break that down. Exactly which of the many things is keeping you quiet?"

Grace gave her a sideways glance, then directed her glance toward the dining room where Charles and granny were deep in conversation.

"Ah." She nodded. "Is something wrong with Charles?"

Grace shrugged. "He gave me a key to his place."

Mom's face lit up. "That's great! Why would you be down about that?"

"He asked for a key to my place."

"Hmm. And I gather you're not ready to commit to that?"

Grace nodded. "I just think things are moving too fast with him. It's not as if we've known each other before. We just met, for christsake."

"Don't cuss." Mom frowned. "Besides, this is the twenty first century. You don't have to date for two years before you sleep with the man. It's just a key, for christsake."

Grace gave her mother a kiss on the cheek. "Don't you start cussing too. You're right, and I'll think about it."

Grace grabbed the lemon meringue pie and followed her mother as they rejoined granny and Charles.

By ten they said their goodnights and used the back door for a quick exit to her apartment.

"So, am I staying here tonight or are you going to break in your new key?" Charles asked once inside her kitchen.

Grace removed the key from her jean pocket and stared at it.

It was shiny and new. Obviously he had it cut especially for her. "Give me a few minutes to pack an overnight bag and get my things for work in the morning."

His face lit up at the prospect of having Grace in his bed tonight as he helped her gather a few things for her overnight stay.

Grace followed him in her car as he took the Toronto bound entrance to the highway.

Where the hell are we going? Grace thought as they picked up speed and passed the Thorold stone road exit.

"I hope he isn't taking me to Toronto," Grace said with slight panic, "I don't want to drive all the way to Toronto."

Grace's panic disappeared as they took the Glendale Avenue turn off and headed toward Niagara on the Lake.

They drove past the local wineries and country-side until they came upon a new subdivision. "Don't tell me he lives in the middle of suburbia," Grace said out loud.

They passed the subdivision and continued down the road another three miles.

Just before the road ended at the main street of Niagara on the Lake, Charles slowed down and put on his right blinker. A hug wrought iron gate opened at the last driveway before the main road.

Charles slowly pulled in, and Grace followed closely behind. She saw the gate slowly close as she cleared the sensors on the gate. She followed Charles up the circular drive and came to a stop in front of a huge white Victorian house. A large dumpster sat to the left of the house filled to the brim with trash.

Grace was taking in the sight, not paying attention, when Charles tapped on her window and opened the car door for her.

"Welcome to my home," he said. "You'll have to excuse the mess. I'm doing some major renovations on the inside, so I'm limited in furniture and some home comforts."

"I thought you lived in an apartment."

Charles gave Grace a puzzled look. "Why would you think I lived in an apartment?"

"I don't know. You just seem like the type who would have some bachelor pad on the main drag where the action is."

He gave out a laugh. "My sweet Grace, you just described yourself."

Grace thought for a moment, then laughed. "You're right. I'm the one with the bachelor pad on the main drag."

"Let me show you around." Grace took her overnight bag from the trunk and handed it to Charles. He took the bag and Grace's hand and led her up the steps to a huge wraparound porch.

Although it was dark outside, Grace could make out a porch swing to the right and some huge potted plants that framed the large double doors. Stained glass graced the front doors, giving it a more authentic Victorian look.

"What beautiful doors. Is the glass original?" Grace asked as her fingers moved over the colored, textured glass.

Grace felt Charles' hands move around her waist, his breath warm against her neck. "Try your key," he whispered.

Grace removed the key from her pocket, slipped it in the lock and gently turned as not to scratch the shiny metal. She heard a click and Charles turned the knob.

"Welcome to my home." He said as he opened the door to reveal a disaster zone.

"It looks like a bomb went off in here," Grace said when he flipped on the hall light.

"Almost," he said apologetically. "I'm not here enough to oversee the workers, so I never know what they've done until I come back at night."

Grace looked around at the piles of rubble that littered almost every part of the main entrance. A narrow path was left to allow access to each room and the grand circular staircase.

"I'm sure it'll look fantastic when it's done," Grace said encouragingly, although at this point she didn't think either of them was too convinced.

Bare bulbs dimly lit each room as he showed Grace around. To the right of the entrance was going to be the formal living room.

To the left was going to be his future den. They walked past the staircase, past a door that led to an unfinished basement, and ended up in the dining room. This room hadn't yet met the workers hammer of destruction.

An antique crystal chandelier hung low over a table, half covered in grey tarp. The ceiling was graced with decorative molding.

"Is that the original molding and chandelier?" Grace asked.

"Based on the photos I found from the original house, I believe it is," he replied.

Grace sighed with relief. "Thank God they didn't touch anything here."

"Yeah. We're using the ceiling as a copy for the other rooms. I didn't want them touching it until they've copied the ceiling exactly."

They moved past the dining room to a great room that worked as the main living space. There was a large kitchen with minimum cupboards and the bare necessities. Next to the kitchen was the family room.

A fifty-two inch flat screen television hung above an ornate marble fireplace. Somehow the television seemed so out of place with the Victorian surroundings.

A black leather sofa that saw better days was covered with blankets and a couple of pillows. Grace got the impression that Charles spent a lot of time sleeping on the sofa.

French doors from the kitchen led out to a glass sunroom. "Come see my hobby," Charles said as he led Grace through the doors.

Once inside the sunroom Grace gasped at the sight of the beautiful exotic plants. In the middle of the room stood a real palm tree sitting comfortably in a huge ceramic pot. It must have been seven feet tall. Colorful orchids lined a large oak table, each pot painted a bright color.

"Someone has a green thumb."

"I love gardening. That's why I bought this place. I have two acres of green to play with." Charles beamed.

He was proud of his plants, and Grace could see why.

Grace, on the other hand could kill silk plants. This was the reason for the lack of greenery in her apartment.

"Why don't you pick out an orchid to take home with you?" Charles suggested.

Grace put her hands up and backed away. "I don't think that would be a good idea, Charles. I'd probably kill it, and they're so beautiful, I wouldn't want anything to happen to it."

Charles gave Grace a sideways look. "Well, okay, if you say so. You can always come here and look at them."

Charles went back into the kitchen and retrieved a bottle of white wine from the fridge. He returned with two plastic disposable cups and the opened bottle of wine.

"Sorry about the crudeness of our first toast in my home, but it's the best I can do for the moment."

Grace smiled and took the cup from him. "That's okay, Charles. There's no need to apologize. Everything is perfect."

Their eyes met and he knew from her smile that Grace meant every word. He returned the smile and moved close enough to gently kiss Grace on the lips.

Grace felt that familiar flutter as his lips brushed against hers.

They stood close together staring out into the night as Charles described his plans for the garden.

"I'm going to make a large koi fish pond with a secret garden that'll be placed just beyond the pool," he said.

"The front will have a four-tiered fountain that will stand in the middle of the circular driveway. That way people visiting will be greeted with the sound of water as they get out of their cars."

"It sounds amazing," Grace said. "How long do you think it'll take to finish the house?"

He thought for a moment. "I guess if I was here every day overseeing the work I could have everything done by thanksgiving." His voice became serious. "But this murder and kidnapping investigation takes up most of my free time."

"Maybe you should hire a contractor to keep an eye on the progress," Grace suggested.

"I have one, but what the house really needs is a woman's touch. Someone who can appreciate the house and see it for its potential beauty."

Grace glanced over at Charles. "Am I being set up here?" she asked, narrowing her eyes slightly.

"That would all depend on what you'd consider a set up." He grinned, not meeting Grace's glance.

"What about your mother? Can't she help you out on this?"

He shook his head. "If I left it up to my mother, she'd tear it down and build a brand new house. I want to turn it back into the house it was when it was first built. Except, of course, with all the new amenities."

"Of course," Grace repeated.

"So what do you think, Grace? Would you be willing to be here every day to make sure the workers don't destroy my place before they fix it?"

Grace sighed deeply. "I don't know, Charles. I have my job, and we're at the beginning of summer, so I need to make the money when I can."

"Your mother and grandmother said they'd take turns to fill in for you."

"You talked to them about this?" Grace took a step back.

"I hope you don't mind," he said. "If talking to them has upset you, I'm sorry. That was never my intention."

It was true, Grace was annoyed. It seemed that he and her family were in cahoots together, and Grace was the last to know.

She was used to being in charge of her own life but since she met Charles, plans were being made without her say. His apology, although sincere, wasn't comforting to Grace.

"I don't like people making decisions about me and my life behind my back. Maybe I should go."

"Please don't go, Grace. Let's forget it, okay? I can hire an interior designer to look after everything. Let's just start over again. Anything you want, but please don't go."

Grace couldn't help but touch his face. His words rang true. He didn't mean to upset her. How could she ever get angry with this wonderful man? He cared enough about her to entrust his prized house to her ideas even though she had none.

"Let me give it some thought, okay? But I can't promise to be here every day."

Charles sighed of relief. "Any time you can spare would be greatly appreciated."

"You've seen my place. Do you honestly think I have a clue on decorating?"

"I trust you."

"Thanks for the vote of confidence but in all reality you should consider hiring an interior as well as a landscape designer. This project is too big and too important to leave to amateurs, let alone me."

He nodded in agreement. "Can you help me find someone?"

Grace laughed at his lost boyish request. "Of course, I can do that. I have a few people in mind who can give you a good price on the work."

The brief moment of tension that quickly filled the air left just as suddenly. Charles showed Grace around the massive house and talked of his plans for the project.

She could picture all his dreams for the house from the main floor to the five bedrooms and four full baths on the second floor. In the master bedroom there's a large balcony that overlooks the grounds.

Grace wanted so much to see the property in the daytime hours. For a moment she wished he would have taken her here during the day instead of night time. But then Grace understood it would be chaotic with workers coming and going and walls being torn down.

It was just past eleven and Grace gave out a yawn. It'd been a long day, and the wine was getting to her. Two glasses and Grace was ready for bed. Anymore than that and she'd be out for the count.

Charles showed Grace to the only bathroom that was functioning, and she locked herself in to shower in private.

Any other night Grace would welcome Charles in the shower with her, but tonight she was too tired to start anything, let alone finish it.

Charles was reading in bed when Grace finally returned to the room.

He'd started a small fire in oversized fireplace, which took the night chill out of the room.

"The furnace isn't working at the moment, so I thought it would be a good idea to have a fire going to keep us warm while we slept."

Grace enjoyed his thoughtfulness and slipped between the sheets next to him.

He stroked her hair as he finished reading. Charles placed his book on the night table, kissed Grace Goodnight, and flicked the light off.

The glow from the fire danced around the room, and they fell asleep in each other's arms to the crackling sound of the burning wood.

SIXTEEN

Grace woke to the sound of hammering outside the window. The sun peeked in through the heavy ornate curtains that barely covered the windows and French doors.

The fire had long since burned itself out, which made the dark room chilly. Grace pulled the covers over her head and closed her eyes. Then it hit her.

She was in Charles' bed, and she was alone. Grace pushed the covers off and hoisted her legs over the side of the bed. She focused on the room to familiarize herself with the surroundings, then walked over to the French doors and pulled the drapes open.

Grace was greeted by the blinding sun and the silhouette of a construction worker standing on a ladder. Grace jumped back, and the worker became startled by Grace's presence.

He grabbed the balcony railing as the ladder started to shake. Grace flung open the doors and reached for his hand to stop him from falling backwards.

"Sorry, ma'am. I didn't realize there's someone sleeping in the room," he said as he steadied himself on the ladder.

Grace looked around the gardens at the beehive of activity. "That's okay. Do you know where Charles is?"

He cocked his head curiously. "Charles?"

"The man who lives here."

"Oh, yeah. He left about fifteen minutes ago."

"Thanks." Grace sighed, then returned to the bedroom, closing the drapes behind her.

Grace threw on Charles' robe and made her way downstairs to the kitchen. The smell of fresh bacon filled her senses, and her stomach growled.

"Great. Just great," Grace mumbled to herself. The first time in his house and he leaves me high and dry with no idea where anything is. Not that it would be difficult to find anything since he hardly has any kitchen cupboards.

Grace found a note on the kitchen counter addressed to her. I was called into the office early. Had some food delivered for you. You can find it in the microwave.

The kettle is ready to be plugged in, and the tea is on the counter. Milk's in the refrigerator. Make yourself at home, and if you are going to work today, don't worry about locking up. The workers know I'm a cop and wouldn't dare steal anything.

A smiley face was followed with love you, Charles.

Grace felt her heart flutter as she read the last sentence.

Does he really love me? Grace thought. It wouldn't be so bad if he did. Grace knew her feelings were becoming deep and serious.

To know that he was feeling the same way, left all that uncertainty out of their relationship. Especially since it was so new and fresh.

Grace tucked the note in the robe pocket and retrieved the breakfast he'd so thoughtfully ordered for her.

After a second cup of tea and a plate full of bacon, biscuits, and fresh fruit, Grace returned to the second floor to shower, dress, and get ready for the day.

It was midweek and Grace decided to take the morning off and explore the grounds of Charles' house. As she walked through the massive property, she envisioned the plans that Charles spoke of.

Cherry trees with a few remaining blossoms, lined a small path that passed the concrete pool.

It was massive and green. Obviously the pool had seen better days. A breeze passed over the fruit trees stealing the remaining pink blooms and carrying them across the open land.

Grace followed the path to a small creek. It was swollen with rain from the past few days, and gathered debris as it flowed under a small bridge and disappeared through some brush.

The sound of activity lined the other side of a juniper lined fence. Grace made her way over to see what was on the other side.

The wrought iron fence separated the property from the street. One side of his property ran along the main road of Niagara on the Lake, and the street was filling up with cars and people.

Some passersby would peer over the fence, trying to get a glimpse of what was on the other side, but the junipers were too tall and thick to allow a good view. Just as well. At least there was privacy from prying eyes.

Grace made her way back to the house and decided to head back to the Falls to catch an early afternoon of work.

She left Charles a note thanking him for the breakfast and asking him to call later when he's free. Grace grabbed her overnight bag, shoved it in the back seat of her car, and drove through the opened gate.

She decided to take a right and drive through the small town and along the parkway back to Clifton Hill. It took longer, but the scenery was spectacular with the Victorian houses and quaint stores that dotted the small main street.

A park sat across from the Prince of Wales Hotel both of which were busy with tourists and locals alike. The farther Grace drove, the less traffic there was until she found herself at a comfortable speed with no one in sight.

Occasionally Grace would pass a parking lot that allowed for people to pull over and soak in the view of the Niagara River. But it was midweek and there weren't as many tourists at this time. Not like on the weekends when the parkway was bumper to bumper.

As Grace passed the floral clock, a feeling of dread came over her. She pulled into the nearest parking lot and shut off the car. Grace tried to shake the terrible feeling of calamity, but couldn't. Grace never felt anything like it before and was compelled to walk the shoreline of the river.

Grace made her way through the thick bush till she found herself in a clearing. The ground was covered in debris, and the view of the United States was lined with factories and abandoned buildings.

She walked up the shore being careful to watch her step as the ground was soft, and there were many fallen branches lying close to the water's edge.

As Grace walked farther up, the panic set in. She wanted to turn back but her heart told her to keep going. Then she saw it. At first Grace wasn't sure what she was seeing, but as she got closer she came to the realization of what she was looking at.

There were branches and leaves covering the body, but the decomposing arm was evident.

"This was the first victim." Grace gasped. "I know it is."

Grace took out her phone and dialed 911. Within minutes the area was cordoned off with yellow caution tape, and police were wandering along the water's edge looking for clues. Grace stood near her car giving a statement when she saw Charles pull up with Sarah riding shotgun.

Grace felt a tinge of jealousy seeing them together, but it quickly disappeared when Charles came to her side and wrapped his arm around her.

"I heard you found a body," he said, kissing Grace on the forehead comfortingly. "Are you okay?"

"I'm a bit shook up, but yes. I think it's the killer's first victim."

"How do you know?" he asked.

"Do you remember the necklace with the J that was found?"

Charles nodded. "You didn't believe it belonged to the girl we found in the area."

"It belongs to this person. I just know it."

Grace took a deep breath as a body bag holding the remains, was hoisted in the back of the coroner's truck.

"Did anyone take your statement yet?" he asked as Sarah moved towards them.

His voice changed from soft to professional. Grace tried not to notice.

"Yes. The officer just finished."

"What were you doing in this area anyway? And what were you doing walking along the shore?" Sarah asked suspiciously.

Grace looked her up and down.

"It's in my statement," Grace replied as she moved closer to Charles. "Just ask the officer, and he'll give you a copy of my statement."

Without responding, she turned on her heels and went in the direction of the officer.

"That was nice," Grace said sarcastically.

"Ignore her. She's just doing her job."

Grace shrugged. "I suppose so."

"Listen, why don't you get out of here and I'll catch up with you later tonight?" Charles suggested.

Grace removed her keys from her pocket. "Good idea. This area gives me the chills."

Grace beeped her car door unlock, and Charles held the door open for her.

He leaned in and gave Grace a long, passionate kiss. "I didn't get a chance to give you one of these this morning." He smiled.

Grace felt that familiar flutter return. "Maybe if you had we wouldn't be here."

He darted his eyes upwards in thought. "You do have a point there. Maybe next time I can."

He moved away from the car and waved as Grace pulled back onto the parkway and turned left toward the Falls.

The farther Grace got from the area, the more she was feeling like her old self. She decided to go straight home and discuss what had happened with her family. They would have more insight on what she'd experienced.

It was late by the time Joe got back to his cottage. He'd been busy with work till the late evening and never had time to look for his next victim. His desires were getting the better of him, and he needed to find a replacement for Becky.

The weekend's coming up. Maybe I'll find someone then, he thought.

He popped a frozen dinner into the microwave, grabbed a beer from the fridge, and flicked on the television to catch the beginning of the news.

They always started with the major story, and he was curious to see if they had any other information on Becky's killer. He choked on his beer as he heard the news crew talk about the discovery of a body.

"How could they have found her? She was hidden so well, and no one ever walks on that area of the shore. It's too fucking close to the water's edge!"

Panic set in, and he didn't know what to do. Should I leave town before they trace her back to me or should I just wait it out and hope for the best? He thought. Neither idea sounded logical.

Leaving would raise suspicions with his business and, if they found out about his relationship with this girl, they'll definitely connect her with him. His mind was going a mile a minute, trying to figure out what to do.

"Damn it!" he screamed. "I should have just buried her body in my yard. No one would have found her."

He paced the floor, rubbing his head, trying to come up with a solution. Then an idea came to him.

He went to the kitchen and retrieved Sarah Child's number from beneath a magnet on the refrigerator. He dialed the number and waited for her to answer. Instead, he got her machine.

"Hey, Sarah. It's me again. Thought I'd call and see if you have some free time we could hook up and have dinner together. Would love to catch up on old times. Thought about you a lot lately."

Joe left his number and hung up the phone. "That should get the ball rolling." He grinned as relief pushed the panic out of his mind.

He knew Sarah all too well. If he played his cards right, it would take him no time at all to get information out of her in regard to the new body. He hatched out his plans and waited for her call.

Sarah unlocked her door and threw her keys in the key dish that sat on a table in the entrance of the small bungalow she shared with her parents. She was still steaming since witnessing her partner's affection toward Grace. She wanted to kick herself for ever suggesting Grace to him. What was she thinking?

All day Charles kept asking her why she was so quiet and distant from him. All she could respond with was she was thinking about the case and how this new body threw a monkey wrench into the information they had so far.

How could she tell him the truth? How could she tell him she wanted him, and she was jealous of seeing him with Grace? She hated him for this. She hated Grace for having what it took to catch Charles. But most of all she hated herself for being jealous.

She had to see Charles every day, and having these feelings was going to make working with him difficult.

"Maybe I can ask for another partner?" she said out loud. "Maybe I can transfer to another city?"

Even if she requested either of these things, they'd take time.

She would still have to see Charles every day, and if he got wind of her plans, she'd have to explain to him why she wanted another partner or wanted to leave Niagara. This would be even more awkward for her.

"I'll just have to stick it out and see how it works." She sighed as she noticed messages on her cell phone.

Three in total. The first two were from her mother asking her about the case.

She zipped through them. The last one she listened to intently. A smile came to her face as she replayed the message.

It was too late to call him back, she thought. She jotted down his number and made a mental note to call him first thing in the morning. "Better yet, I'll stop by and see him before he heads out for lunch." She smiled.

The anger and jealousy she was feeling all day suddenly left her. She was feeling better since the message from her ex boyfriend.

She headed for the bathroom, stripped, and turned on the shower. Maybe her life wasn't so shit after all. Maybe rekindling things with him was exactly what she needed.

SEVENTEEN

"I don't know what was wrong with Sarah all day," Charles said as Grace crawled in next to him.

"I saw the way she looked at you, Charles."

He gave Grace a puzzled look. "What do you mean by that?"

"What I mean is that I think she's hoping for something more with you than just being partners at work."

He smiled. "You think so?"

Grace narrowed her eyes. "Don't even think about it!"

Charles gave out a hearty laugh wrapped his arms around Grace and pulled her close. "I'm a one-woman man. And you're the only woman for me." He kissed her ear, then her cheek and ended up on Grace's lips.

"Hmm. I like the sound of that," Grace whispered as she felt her body melt from his touch.

"Why don't we christen my bedroom?" He smiled.

"You mean to say that you haven't done anything with anyone in this room yet?"

He shook his head. "Nope."

"How long have you been living here?"

He thought for a moment. "About a year."

"And in all that time, you haven't had sex?"

Charles moved away and pulled the covers over his chest. "I didn't say that."

"But you've never brought a woman here to spend the night."

Charles propped his head up with his hand, eyes focused on Grace. "I've had a few dates since I moved here but nothing serious. Some I've spent the night with at their place, but I'd never bring anyone to my home to spend the night unless I had deep feelings for them"

A smile formed on Grace's lips, and she leaned in to kiss him. "Good answer." Grace laughed as she pulled the blankets over their heads.

She stopped for a moment. "Does that mean you have deep feelings for me?"

Joe handed Sarah a hamburger and drink, and they took their food to a table far from prying ears.

"Thanks for the phone call last night," Sarah said as she sipped her Coke. "It was exactly what I needed after the day I had."

Joe smiled. "My pleasure. I was meaning to call you before, but now that tourist season is here, I get pretty busy and lose track of time."

Sarah nodded in agreement. "I know what you mean. I've wanted to stop by to say hi while you're working but with this murder case going on, I haven't had time for anything."

"You're involved in the case of the killings?" he asked nonchalantly.

Sarah nodded. "Yeah. We found another body yesterday."

Joe leaned back in his seat. "Wow! How many does that make so far?"

"So far we've linked four bodies to the same person, but we aren't sure yet if this one is linked to the others, so I'm not going to speculate."

"Between us, do you think they're related?"

Sarah looked around as if to check for anyone listening in. "Between you and me, I think they are. And if she is then based on the composition of the body, she may have been his first victim."

Joe moved in closer. "What makes you think it's the same killer?"

"She was found on the shore of the Niagara River, hidden by debris."

"But?" Joe asked.

"But there were no reports of anyone missing, and it looked like someone deliberately concealed the body."

Joe tried to act surprised. "That's a lot to think about."

Sarah nodded. "It's obvious the body met with foul play, but how the body was disposed of wasn't the same as the others. It's going to be difficult to link her to the others."

Joe finished his lunch in silence, but his mind was going a mile a minute. He was glad that he took Jenny's necklace and threw it over the cliff near the water. He wasn't sure if they found the necklace, but it'd been a long time, and there'd been plenty of rain for it to be buried in the mud if it didn't land in the water. But he had to know for sure.

"If you aren't doing anything Friday night, maybe we can have dinner together and see a movie later?" he asked.

Sarah's face lit up at his proposal. "Lunch, now dinner and a movie all in one week? I'd love to!" she giggled like a school girl.

Her giggle irritated the hell out of Joe, bringing back one of the reasons he dumped her in the first place. He just smiled through it, then took her hand and kissed it.

"I missed you, Sarah," he said convincingly.

She cupped his hand in hers. "I missed you, too, darling."

She leaned in to kiss him and was interrupted by the ringing of her cell phone. She held up a finger to Joe as she answered the phone.

"Where are you?" Charles asked.

"I'm having lunch with a friend," she replied. "What's up?"

"Meet me at the office. We have an I.D. on the body we found."

"Any coroner's report yet?" she asked, trying to sound important in front of Joe.

"Not yet. Just the I.D.," Charles answered.

"Okay. I'll be there in fifteen minutes." She closed her phone and put it back in her pocket.

"Duty calls," she said as she finished the last of her burger and drink.

"What was that all about?" Joe asked.

"That was my partner. We have a name to go with that body we found." Sarah gathered the trays and dumped the paper plates and empty cups in the trash. She placed the trays on top of the cans and turned to Joe.

"Are we still on for Friday night?" she asked.

"Of course we are." He smiled. "Wouldn't miss it for the world."

She leaned in and kissed him. Joe welcomed her kiss and reciprocated by pulling her close. "I'll call you later," he said.

They parted ways, and Joe watched Sarah disappear in the crowd of people on Clifton Hill. He sat down and was overwhelmed with panic.

They know who she is, he thought. It's just a matter of time before they link her with me, then they'll link the other ones with me, too.

Be cool, he thought to himself. If they come knocking and asking questions about Jen, just play dumb. You can tell them that she was into kinky sex and that you broke it off with her because she was getting too intense.

You can tell them that you hadn't seen her since you broke it off. The panic was replaced with relief. Yup. That's what I'll do. I'll just play dumb.

"What do we have?" Sarah asked Charles.

"Her name is Jennifer Smythe. No next of kin that we're aware of." He handed her a copy of the report on Jennifer Smythe.

"She was arrested for prostitution about two years ago. That's how we were able to identify her so quickly," Charles said.

"She worked as an exotic dancer down at one of the strip clubs on the outskirts of town." She read aloud. "Have you checked out her last known address yet?"

"Was just about to do that. Want to come along?"

"You bet I do," she said, grabbing her purse. "You drive. I'll ride shot gun."

Ten minutes later they were parked on Bridge Street, outside a slightly rundown apartment complex that saw better days.

Bridge Street consisted of three story apartment buildings and Victorian houses that were turned into duplexes and triplexes. Most came furnished and most tenants never stayed longer than a few months. They either ended up in jail or dead.

Bridge Street was well known for prostitution and drug activity by the police and the local residents. Most of the prostitutes and pimps lived in the area as well as the major drug dealers.

Over the years the city did what they could to clean up the area especially during the summer months when the city was flocked with tourists. But it was always business as usual.

During the winter, prostitution and drug deals were taken indoors when the weather was too cold for anyone to venture outdoors.

Charles and Sarah stood at the landlord's door discussing Jennifer Smythe. Based on her appearance, she looked as if she'd fallen on hard times most of her life.

A cigarette hung from her dry lips, and occasionally an ash would fall from the end as she spoke. Her hair was thick and grey, and her breath was the combination of liquor and cigarettes.

"I don't make it a habit to interfere in the comings and goings of my tenants," she said.

"We aren't asking you that. All we want to know is when was the last time you saw Miss Smythe?" Sarah asked.

The woman thought for a moment. "Like I said, I keep my nose out of my tenants' business. I don't care how they make money just as long as they pay their rent on time."

Sarah was getting frustrated with the old woman and was about to lose it on her when Charles intervened.

"I respect that, ma'am," he said. "It must be difficult to manage a place this size and to know all your tenants personally, but any information you can give us would be greatly appreciated." He smiled his model smile and gave her a wink. This brought a toothless grin to the woman's lips.

"Well, I remember her, alright. She didn't stay here long. She lived here for about six months then gave me two months notice because she was moving. As a matter of fact I still have some of her stuff in storage. She left and never came back." She took a key from the wall in her entranceway and motioned for Sarah and Charles to follow her.

They took the stairs to the basement where there was a row of storage doors for each apartment. Most were empty except for a few seasonal things such as bikes and sleds. She unlocked the storage door for apartment 6J.

"This is all the stuff she left behind in her apartment. The new tenant hasn't asked for the stuff to be moved from his storage space yet. Not that he'd need it. He had one suitcase when he moved in."

She stepped aside while Charles and Sarah examined Jennifer's sparse belongings.

"No furniture?" Sarah asked.

"The apartments come fully furnished. I suppose I should find another place for her things," she added.

The woman looked at her watch. "Exactly how long do you think you'll be here?" she asked impatiently. "My soap's coming on soon, and I don't want to miss it."

"We can lock up after we're finished," Charles offered. "There's really no need for you to be here."

She pressed her lips together and tapped her chipped painted nail on her watch. "I suppose it'll be alright as long as you promise to lock up."

"No problem," Charles said.

The woman turned and headed back toward the stairs, then stopped suddenly. "You never told me what Jennifer did," she asked.

"She didn't do anything. Her body was discovered on the shore of the Niagara River," Sarah said without looking up.

"Oh," the woman responded without changing her tone, then disappeared up the stairs.

Charles and Sarah looked up in time to see her exit through the stairway.

"Sounds concerned to me," Sarah said sarcastically.

Charles nodded in agreement, then went back to searching through the meager belongings.

"Doesn't look like she had much of anything here. Even her clothes were limited," Charles said.

"Something seems strange about that," Sarah said.

"I know what you mean. If she was a dancer, she should have some costumes here."

"Do you suppose she had another place?" Sarah asked.

"Could be. Maybe they have some information at the club she danced at," Charles said.

They were about to give up when they came across a worn address book and a small photo album.

"These might come in handy," Charles said as he put them aside. "I think we've found all that we could possibly use."

He replaced the padlock and clicked it shut. They moved up the stairs and out the front door without notice from the landlady. They placed the property in the trunk of the car and headed back to the office.

"If she was arrested for prostitution, I think it would be a good idea to talk to some of the girls on Bridge Street," Sarah said. "I'm sure they might know some of Jennifer's regulars."

It was too early for the girls. Most came out as soon as the sun went down for fear of being spotted by the cops. Some would linger in doorways and step out when a car would cruise the street looking for a date or a fix. If an agreement was established the car would pull over and the John would follow the girl to her apartment where business would be taken care of.

This made it safe for the girls and private for the Johns, away from the cops.

Love and Murder on the Hill

"Let's head to the club. It shouldn't be too busy at this time." Charles suggested.

Grace closed up shop to take an hour lunch. Marco and Aaron waved Grace over to join them. She always refused their offer, but after her brief time with Marco, she felt more comfortable about joining the partners for lunch.

Aaron had always been the geeky kid in school. He weighed ninety pounds soaking wet until he was eighteen. Puberty kicked in and God was good.

He had everything in all the right places and the brains to go with it. Yes God was definitely shining down on him when he developed chest hair. He's been dating the same girl since high school.

Emma was a geek like Aaron but she still looked the part. That didn't change Aaron's feelings for her. They plan to get married next spring.

Aaron and Marco each locked an arm in Grace's and the three of them walked down to Clifton Hill to taste one of the fast food delicacies that were abundant on the Hill.

"You're looking mighty fine today Grace if I do say so myself," Aaron said as they walked down the street.

"Nice of you to notice," Grace replied with a smile.

"Didn't you hear Aaron? Grace has a new boyfriend, and from what I heard he's a good looking cop," Marco said.

"Is that so?" Aaron asked.

Grace blushed slightly and nodded in agreement.

"So that's what I've been noticing about you lately?" Aaron said. "You've been getting some."

Grace did a mental eye roll. "What is it with guys?"

She stopped herself. "Never mind. I don't want to know."

They ducked into the burger joint next to the funhouse and found a seat by the window. Aaron took down orders and took his place in line.

"I'm glad you came out with us Grace," Marco said. "We've been working across from each other for a few years now and we never talk."

"I figured it was time for me to let go of the past and move on," Grace replied. "We're all adults now and we need to watch each other's back while we work the Hill."

"Speaking of watching each other's back. Me and Aaron have been giving it some thought on this nutcase who's been going around snatching women off the street and killing them," Marco said.

Aaron joined the table and divided up the food.

"So what's your theory on this?" Grace asked.

"We think it's someone who works the Hill." Aaron joined in. "Someone who's attractive and in a position to talk up the tourists."

"Anyone in mind?" Grace asked.

Marco shrugged. "Well, that's just it. We can't figure out who it could be."

"We first thought it could be someone at a night club, but the last girl was only eighteen so he wouldn't have met her there," Aaron said.

"That's when we came up with the idea of someone on the Hill." Marco added.

Grace thought for a moment. "It makes sense. Some of the girls were visiting the area. They must have met someone in one of the shops or restaurants on the Hill or Lundy's Lane."

"Maybe we can do our own investigation?" Aaron suggested.

"Yeah we could be the Hardy Boys and Grace can be our Moll," Marco said.

"How come I have to be the Moll? Why can't I be Nancy Drew?"

"Okay fine. You can be Nancy Drew, but I think you would make a much better Moll," Marco replied.

"What's a Moll anyway?" Grace asked.

Aaron shrugged. "Beats the hell out of me."

EIGHTEEN

The trio finished their lunch, threw the wrappers and cups in the trash and ushered out the door. The sun was in full summer heat and the humidity was rising from the pavement as people searched for a shady place to relax.

The sound of music blared along the Hill as someone did their best karaoke imitation of Madonna.

"What the hell is that?" Aaron asked, holding his hands over his ears.

"If I didn't know better, I would think some cat is stuck in a squeaky gate," Grace said.

Marco moaned. "That's the new karaoke bar on the Rooftop café."

"Karaoke bar?" Aaron and Grace said together.

Marco nodded. "It was Smedley's idea. He thought it would be a great place to have a karaoke bar for all ages."

"You mean to say we're gonna listen to this every day?" Grace asked. "How am I going to focus on my readings with that blaring all day?"

"I'm afraid so," Marco said. "It's become a hit with all the tourists as well as the locals."

"I hear they serve the best chicken wings," Aaron said adding his two cents worth.

"There's got to be some noise ordinance," Grace said. "I'm going to find out if there's some kind of law against excessive noise."

"If there isn't, there should be a law against public torture of a really good song." Marco laughed.

Sarah sat in the passenger seat of Charles' car, looking through the photo album they found in Jennifer Smythe's belongings. She came upon a recent photo of Jennifer, removed it from the plastic and placed it in her jacket pocket.

"In case she used a different name," she said.

Charles turned up Stanley Avenue and made a right on Lundy's Lane. He drove past Grace's house and glanced quickly.

Sarah pretended not to notice.

They kept driving until they were on the outskirts of the city. A few exotic clubs were situated along the vacant land.

As much as they tried to make them look high class and sophisticated, they were nothing more than glorified strip clubs. The police were called numerous times to intervene between drunken patrons and the girls.

The bouncers could only do so much before the arguments turned into full blown fist fights.

The gentlemen's club, as it was called, was the least troublesome. Maybe it had to do with the name or maybe it had to do with the fact that the bouncers were cops who wanted to make a little extra money by moonlighting.

Either way, if it was compared to the other places, it would come out on top as the high class strip club in the area.

Charles wheeled his car into the parking lot and stopped short of the main doors. A couple of cars and a van were the only sign of it being open. Probably the cleaning crew and manager, he thought.

They walked into the front door and stopped for a moment to adjust their vision. The place was huge and dark except for the moving lights that lit up the dance floor.

Chairs lined the 'T' shaped dance floor for a front row view of the ladies. The rest of the place was wall to wall tables and chairs. The mile-long mirrored bar stood half the length of the room.

A balding, short, round man stood behind the bar looking over some paperwork. He was totally oblivious to Charles and Sarah until they walked over and showed their badges.

"Hey, we're closed. Whatever you want can wait till we open." He grumbled at the sight of the two detectives.

"We're not here to talk about your business," Charles said.

"We want to ask you about a girl who worked here."

Sarah showed him the picture, and the man took it with his chubby fingers.

He studied the photo. "What's this all about?"

"Do you know her?" Charles asked.

"That would all depend," he said, handing the photo back to Sarah.

The partners looked at each other.

"That would depend on what?" Sarah asked.

"It would depend on what this has to do with my club."

Charles leaned in and grabbed the guy by his greasy dress shirt. "Do I have to look around for violations or are you going to answer our question?"

The man pulled away and put his hands up in surrender. "Okay, okay. I was just joking. Sure, I know her. That's Precious but I haven't seen her for months."

"Is that the name she uses on stage or the name she used to get hired?" Charles asked.

"I don't know her full name. I have too many girls to remember everyone's name, and they come and go here too fast. So it's easier to call them by their stage name."

"Did she have any regulars who ask for her specifically?"

"All the girls have regulars. But I do remember Precious had a boyfriend."

"Tell us about the boyfriend," Sarah said.

"The owner thought for a moment. "Don't know much about him except that a few times Precious would come in complaining about him."

Their attention was distracted by some women who came into the club.

The man waved them over. "Look, you'd do better asking the girls. They spend a lot of time gossiping between sets. If anyone knows anything, one of them would."

"Thanks for your time," Charles said, and the two of them motioned for the girls to sit at a table.

"I liked that good cop bad cop routine you just pulled," Sarah whispered.

Charles just smiled.

They showed Jennifer's photo, but they were new there and hadn't met her.

"Are you girls old enough to be doing this sort of work?" Sarah asked.

The pretty petite blonde laughed. "We're all twenty. Want to see our I.D.?"

Charles shook his head. "All of you should be in school getting an education."

The three girls looked at each other and giggled. "We're in school. University is out for the summer."

Both partners' eyes went wide.

"Is this what you do when you aren't in school?" Sarah asked.

"We make more money here in one weekend than we can make down in the tourist trap selling junk food," the blonde responded. "Besides, we need to pay for our education somehow."

Charles felt as if they were at a dead end with the girls and thanked them for their help.

The girls stood and offered a free lap dance to Charles if he wanted to come back later. "Thanks, ladies, but I'm seeing someone." He smiled.

"Bring her with you. We can do you both." They laughed.

"If I did she'd probably kill me."

"Thanks for your help," Sarah said smugly. "We need to get going."

The girls looked her up and down, then turned their attention back to Charles. "We'll be here if you ever change your mind," the blonde said as they crossed the floor and disappeared through the door that led to their dressing room.

"Well, that was a waste of time," Sarah said.

"Not really. If these girls have been here for a few months and didn't know Jennifer, it would mean she'd been missing before April when university is out for the summer."

They thanked the owner and were about to leave when one of the girls reappeared from the back room and headed their way.

"I have something for you," the dark haired girl said. She handed them a name, address, and phone number. "This girl's been working here the longest. If anyone would know her, she would." She quickly hurried back to the dressing room without waiting for a response.

Charles looked at the paper. "Missy Maxwell," he read aloud.

"Missy Maxwell?" Sarah repeated. "I know that girl!" We went to high school together. Last I heard she moved to New York to go to school. I didn't know she was back in town."

"Well, I guess you know what she was studying." Charles laughed.

Sarah narrowed her eyes at her partner. "That's not funny. She actually went to study dance. She was a fantastic dancer. She took tap, jazz, and ballet all through her childhood. Who would have thought she'd end up stripping for drunken old men?" Sarah blew out a sigh at what became of her school friend.

She shook her head in disbelief. "What a shame. She was so talented."

Charles put a supporting arm around his partner. It was obvious that this news upset her greatly, but all he could do was listen. He was at a loss for words on how to comfort Sarah. "Maybe we should pay her a visit?" he suggested.

"If you wouldn't mind, I'd prefer to bow out of this. I don't think I have the heart to face her. She might be embarrassed by my presence."

"I understand," Charles replied as he held the door for his partner. "I'll drop you off at the office. Call if you need me," he added.

He dropped Sarah off and punched in Missy's address in his G.P.S.

He thought it would be better to meet with her in person than on the phone.

He took the highway toward Fort Erie and exited on Montrose Road. He turned right and followed the G.P.S. until it brought him to a small cul-de-sac of thirty-year-old bungalows. Hard to believe a stripper lives in this area, Charles thought. But then again, nothing should surprise me anymore since meeting three students who make their tuition stripping.

Missy lived in a small bungalow situated at the end of the street. Her house was modest yet beautifully cared for. Freshly planted annuals lined the sidewalk and driveway as well as the edge of the small rose garden.

Charles took note of the license plate of the only car in the driveway as he walked up the steps to a cement porch that spanned the distance of the front of the house. He rang the door bell and waited.

Nothing. He rang it again. Still nothing. It was mid afternoon. Maybe she's out? He thought. If she was, then whose car was that in the driveway?

He was about to leave when the inside door opened. "Sorry, didn't hear the doorbell. I was in the back yard planting flowers."

"Are you Missy Maxwell?" Charles asked the tall thin brunette.

"Who wants to know?"

Charles pulled out his badge and information. "Niagara Falls Police. I want to ask you a few questions about Jennifer Smythe."

Missy opened the screen door and motioned Charles inside.

"Have a seat. I've been wondering where she went to. I still have some of her costumes and clothes here." Missy poured two glasses of fresh lemonade and handed one to Charles.

"Freshly squeezed," she said as she sat across from him at her small kitchen table.

Charles took a sip and and gave a smile of approval. He watched Missy unwrap her long hair, gather the loose strands, then neatly tie her hair back in a pony tail.

"You said you have some of her belongings?"

Missy nodded. "Yeah. She asked me to hold onto them for her while she moves."

"To Bridge Street?"

She shook her head and laughed. "She was moving out of that dump and in with her boyfriend. I thought she might have left town instead."

"She had a boyfriend? Do you know his name?" Charles waited to jot down any information Missy had for him.

"Sorry, can't help you on that one, but she did say he worked on the Hill. But I don't know what he did."

"You said you thought she might have left town instead of moving in with the boyfriend," Charles asked. "Why would you think that?"

"It wasn't a secret that the boyfriend had a temper.

Jennifer complained a few times about him man handling her and leaving bruises," Missy said.

"Then why would she want to move in with him?"

"I've got no clue," Missy said. "Jen always said in spite of the roughness, he was the best thing that ever happened to her. I told her she was crazy to stay with some guy who laid his hands on her."

"What about her family?" Charles asked. "Did she ever mention her family to you?"

"Look, detective, if she didn't tell me her boyfriend's name, what makes you think she would mention her family? All I know is that she had no family. The only thing she told me about her life was she came from a small farming area up north somewhere."

Charles put his pad and pen back in his jacket pocket. "Would it be okay if I take a look at her things?"

"Knock yourself out." Missy showed him the room where she kept Jennifer's belongings.

"I need to shower and get ready for work," Missy said, looking at her watch. "Would you be able to let yourself out when you're finished?"

"No problem," Charles said.

Missy turned to leave the room, then stopped in the doorway and turned back to Charles. "You never told me why you're looking for Jennifer."

"We aren't looking for her. We're investigating her murder," Charles said.

Missy felt her heart drop in her stomach. "She's dead?" She felt herself become light-headed and her knees weakened. She held the wall as she covered her eyes in shock.

Charles grabbed her just before she fainted and helped her to the bed.

A few minutes later Missy regained consciousness and saw Charles sitting next to her while two paramedics brought in a stretcher.

"I don't need an ambulance," she protested.

"You fainted and were out for awhile," Charles replied.

"You should go to the hospital to be checked out."

"I'm fine. I just had too much sun working out in the yard all morning."

She shooed one of the paramedics away as he tried to take her blood pressure. "Ma'am, please let me do my job," he insisted.

Charles handed Missy a glass of water. "Let them check you out, okay?"

Missy nodded, sipped her water, and let the paramedics do what they needed to do so they would leave her in peace.

After they checked her over, they gave Charles a nod of approval and didn't see any reason to take her to the hospital. They did suggest she see her family doctor as soon as possible.

She promised she would, and Charles saw the paramedics to the door. He thanked them for their time and told them to send any charges to the Niagara Falls Police.

He returned to the room to check on Missy. "Maybe you should take a couple of days off."

She shook her head. "No can do. I need to work now before I start to show."

"Huh? What?"

"I'm pregnant, and I need to work now before I start getting bigger. I won't be able to dance when I'm eight months pregnant." She laughed.

"If you don't mind me asking, where's the father? Does he know?"

"No. He doesn't know, and I don't want him to know either," she said. "The last thing I need is to have some man whore in my life trying to play father to my child."

"I think he has a right to know. Besides, he should help support the child," Charles replied.

Missy thought for a moment. "Maybe you're right. But I'm financially secure enough to look after the baby on my own. My house is paid for, and I have money put away for when I retire. I even have plans to open a dance studio one day."

"Regardless, you still should let him know," Charles insisted.

Missy smiled and nodded. "I'll think about it."

She got to her feet and held her breath. No dizziness. "Okay, now I'm off to shower."

She turned to Charles and kissed him on the cheek. "Thanks for your concern. And I'm truly sorry to hear about Jennifer. If you find out anything, would you let me know? I didn't know her that well, but what I did know of her I liked. She was a good person. She just had a few bad breaks in her life."

Charles handed her his card and told her to call if she remembers anything that might help. He promised to lock up before he left and went back to the boxes that held Jennifer's belongings.

Missy took his card and disappeared down the hall. The faint sound of water running followed a few minutes later.

Charles went through the boxes of clothes and dance outfits. He checked the pockets of all the pants and jackets, but found nothing of importance. He was about to give up when at the bottom of the last box he came across a piece of scrap paper with a phone number scribbled across it. A small heart was drawn around the number.

Must be Jennifer's handwriting, he thought.

He took out his cell and dialed the number. It was no longer in service.

Charles put all the belongings back in the boxes, turned the lock on the front door as he left, and got into his car.

He called dispatch and asked them to find information on the number he found.

"May take some time," the dispatch operator said.

"No problem," Charles replied. "Call my cell when you find out."

He started his car and headed toward Lundy's Lane.

NINETEEN

Grace was busy in her kitchen when Charles arrived at the door. "Nice to see you," she said, greeting him with a kiss.

Her smile disappeared as she sensed something was bothering him. "What's wrong?"

He went to the fridge and grabbed a soda. "Do you know a woman named Missy Maxwell?"

"Yeah, I went to school with her. She chummed around with Sarah during high school. Why do you ask?"

"Sarah told me the same thing. We found out that she's dancing in the area."

"Really? Which ballet company is she with? She's an amazing dancer. I'd love to see her professionally."

"It's not ballet, and if you want to see her dance professionally, you shouldn't go alone."

Grace was confused. "What do you mean?"

"She's not with any ballet company. She's stripping at the gentlemen's club on the outskirts of town."

Grace felt the blood leave her face and her heart jump into her throat. "You're kidding, right?"

"Sarah had the same reaction," Charles said. "Was she really that good that she could be a professional ballet dancer?"

"She didn't like me," Grace said. "But I still admired her talent. She was just as good as the professional dancers on television. What the hell could have happened for her to end up stripping?"

Charles shrugged. "Who knows?"

Grace sat at the kitchen table mulling over this new revelation.

"There's something else," Charles said.

"There's more?"

He nodded. "Apparently she's pregnant by some guy who works on Clifton Hill."

"Did she tell you who it was?"

"Nope. She just said that he's a bit of a ladies' man, and she didn't want him to know."

Grace's heart went out to Missy. Although they were never friends, she was gifted, and Grace had hoped to see her fulfill her dreams. "I guess having my own gift makes me more sensitive to others who are gifted in other ways," Grace said.

"If it's any consolation, she seems happy. She owns her own home, and she has plans to open a dance studio someday soon." Charles said trying to lighten the mood.

"I suppose that does make up for her crushed dreams." Grace sighed. "I must contact her when all this is over."

It was early Saturday morning, and the Hill was abuzz with activity. It was also the first weekend of July, and school was officially out for the summer. The borders were already bumper to bumper with traffic from the U.S. as their Fourth of July and Canada Day fell on the same long weekend.

Grace was busy setting up, and already had people standing around waiting for a reading. It'll definitely be a busy day, she thought. She would have to keep the readings short. No embellishing today.

Aaron and Marco were already in the swing of things by trying to coax tourists into trying their strength or their agility and speed climbing the rock wall.

Grace watched out of the corner of her eye as Marco would occasionally stop and wave to her.

Aaron was helping a couple of young kids climb the wall by directing them to the right pegs. They squealed with delight and waved to their parents as they reached the top. Pictures were taken as the small audience clapped with approval at their accomplishment.

"You made it in record time," Aaron would say as he unhooked their safety harnesses. He always had special prizes for the little ones.

He'd make a great father, Grace thought, as she watched how patient he was with the children. He'd encourage them and praise them. Occasionally he'd too wave over at Grace as if to say hello.

The three of them became close friends over the past two weeks. They spent their lunches comparing thoughts on the serial killer. Each lunch left them at a dead end.

It'd been a few weeks since the discovery of Jennifer's body. There'd been no missing person's reports and no discoveries of other bodies. It was as if the killer had vanished.

According to Charles, Sarah had changed, too. He said she seemed different, as if she may have someone in her life. She wasn't rolling her eyes as much when he mentioned Grace's name. That gave Grace some sense of relief when it came to them being partners.

Another thing that changed was Grace. She found herself spending more and more time at Charles' place. Grace helped him find an interior decorator that specialized in restoring old Victorian houses to their former glory. She researched his house and found photographs of some of the interior and exterior.

Charles did make some small modifications as to color and wallpaper, but stayed in keeping with the ornate ceilings and carved wooden balusters. He didn't change a thing as far as the exterior was concerned except for new windows and maintenance free siding that looked like wood.

He had plans to have the place finished inside and out in time for Christmas. He wanted to have both their families there for a huge Christmas celebration. Grace suggested he take it one day at a time.

Christmas was far away, and anything could happen between now and then. He dismissed her suggestion and stayed with his plans.

"You're not going anywhere," he'd say. "This is your home, too." His words always touched Grace, but she was a realist, and in her world, gypsy women never married the father of their child.

Not that Grace was planning on getting pregnant anytime soon, but if she was, she definitely wanted Charles to be the father.

Grace wasn't as optimistic about their future as he was, so she just went along with him and kept her thoughts to herself.

Yes, everything in Grace's life seemed to be almost perfect. All the planets and stars were aligned perfectly. Then why did Grace have this overwhelming feeling that the axe was about to fall?

Charles was at a stalemate with the investigation. The information he had on Jennifer's boyfriend was at a dead end. Either people didn't know her or they weren't talking.

He found this sort of loyalty amongst the Hill workers unusual.

The regulars who worked the Hill were like the freaks at the carnival side show. It was as if they were a family unit, and family never squealed on other family members.

He asked for Grace's help, so she kept her ears and eyes open without looking too obvious, but the Hill was small. Everyone knew everyone's business.

Grace was the new topic on the Hill. She was dating the detective in charge of the murder investigation. Because of this they began to keep Grace at arm's length.

Not that Grace wanted to be a part of their little group anyway. But being accepted was a lot easier on the Hill than being an outcast. And Grace was all too familiar with playing that role.

Grace tried not to let this bother her. As thick as she thought her skin was, there were a few thin spots that remarks would get through to. Grace tried to ignore the remarks and continued with her daily routine.

Although dating a cop made it difficult to find out anything on her own, she wasn't alone in her quest for answers. She developed a close friendship with Aaron and Marco. The Hill people liked them. Because of this they were able to ask questions and move freely without suspicion.

Every evening they'd get together and pool their information and ideas. So far they eliminated most of the obvious people. They too were feeling as if they were at a stalemate.

The summer brought more than just tourists to Clifton Hill. It brought hot, humid weather and a sense of uneasiness among the locals. A killer was loose, and the police weren't any further ahead in capturing this person as they were a month ago.

Politicians were also fed up with the snail's pace that the investigation was going. The mayor wanted this killer caught before there was another murder while Niagara Falls was in full tourist mode. But by all accounts, that wouldn't be possible.

The mayor threatened to bring in the R.C.M.P. on the case, but Charles wasn't annoyed by that. Any extra help would be a welcome sight for their small division. They were undermanned since most uniformed officers were patrolling the street to keep things under control with the daily arrival of visitors.

The casinos were packed to capacity, and every hotel in the city was booked weeks in advance. Summer was definitely a booming business for Niagara Falls and the Hill.

Once the sun went down Grace would pack up her belongings, have a short meeting with Aaron and Marco, then drive the distance to Charles' house. It had gotten to a point that Grace moved most of her clothing into the extra closet he had reserved for her.

Grace enjoyed staying at the house, especially since the nights were unusually hot and he had the salt water pool up and running. They'd take a dip late in the evening when the streets were void of people.

It was the first time Grace had ever done it in a pool and, knowing their track record, it wouldn't be the last. They were like rabbits when it came to sex. Grace looked at the pool in a different way now.

They began christening every room in his house. Even the ones that were still in construction mode. Everywhere Grace looked she had a warm feeling of love and sex. His presence was everywhere, even when he wasn't there. Grace loved his house.

The sun was beginning to disappear behind the buildings that lined the Hill. Grace called it a night and began packing her belongings to make the drive to Charles' house.

Grace was putting her cooler and umbrella in the trunk of the car when she felt the breath of someone on the back of her neck. Grace turned around quickly and was nose to nose with Marco.

"Seeing that we're not having our usual meeting tonight, do you want to go out for a drink?" he asked with a smile.

Grace slammed the trunk and blinked the car unlock.

"Thanks, but no thanks. I'm tired, and my brain is fried from all the readings. I just want to go home and veg," Grace said as she slid in to the driver's side and turned the key.

Marco felt slighted. "Maybe next time?" he asked.

Grace put the car in gear. "For sure next time Marco. I promise."

Marco gave her a thumbs up, tapped the roof of the car and gave her a wave.

On that note Grace drove out of the lot and maneuvered her car through the hoards of people.

Aaron walked over to where Marco was standing. "She's in love," Aaron said.

"Yep she sure is," Marco replied.

Aaron threw his arm around his friends shoulder. "Well, if it doesn't work out with her and the cop, maybe you can have a second chance."

"Maybe," Marco said.

They walked over to Aaron's car and Aaron beeped the doors unlock. Aaron slid behind the wheel as Marco climbed into the passenger seat. "If it's any consequence Marco, you still got me." Aaron smiled.

"At least I got the booby prize if not the boobies." Marco laughed.

Aaron started his car and tore out of the parking lot, nearly running down some Asian tourists who walked in front of him.

He laid on the horn, and they jumped out of the way. A few words were exchanged, none of which should be repeated. He inched his car onto Clifton Hill and blended with the rest of the traffic.

TWENTY

Sarah hurried home to shower and change. Her date would be picking her up around ten for a late supper and dancing afterwards. She washed her hair and dried it down, allowing her red hair to fall freely over her shoulders. Tonight she hoped would be the night for her.

She'd been seeing her high school sweetheart for a couple of weeks and until now things only went as far as heavy kissing and petting. But tonight Sarah wanted more. She had secretly arranged a room at one of the honeymoon hotels. She chose a room with a fireplace and jacuzzi for two.

Sarah had already picked up the key and paid for everything in advance. No time to waste tonight, she thought. She even arranged for a bottle of wine to be chilling when they arrived.

Yes, tonight was going to be the night. She needed it. Sarah always had a special place in her heart for her first love. During school they never went all the way, and there were times during her adult life that she fantasized about what it would be like.

When he called her she felt like a school girl again.

She walked with a bouncy step. She caught herself singing for no apparent reason, and she carried a permanent smile on her face.

Even when Charles mentioned Grace, it didn't seem to bother her as much as before. Her life was definitely falling into place. The only thing she needed to do now was get a place of her own.

Although she loved her parents, she found her mother quite smothering. She was a grown woman and a police detective to boot. Yet her mother found it necessary to call her several times a day to find out where she was

Catherine Angelone

or when she'd be home. She even called during investigations to tell her that supper would be ready soon and if they should start without her.

Sarah definitely needed a place of her own. She made a mental note that first thing tomorrow she'd start looking for a condo or small house to buy. After all, she did have enough money saved to give a substantial down payment. Sarah picked out a black lace bra and matching thong. This should turn him on, she thought as she slipped the panties on. She wore a short black skirt and pink tank top under a sheer white blouse. The outfit showed her curves, and it would allow easy access while driving.

As Grace drove down the parkway toward Niagara on the Lake, she got this overwhelming feeling that she was being followed. There were many cars on the road so Grace couldn't know for sure. But her instincts are sensitive and they told her someone was following her back to Charles's house.

Grace decided to take a few extra turns to look as if she was stopping to pick up some things. As Grace turned down a residential street, she noticed a car, four car lengths behind her, do the same thing.

Grace knew there was a corner store close by, so she'd pull in and pick up milk. If Grace was being followed, this person may follow her into the parking lot.

Grace pulled into the lot, careful to park close enough to the door in case anything were to happen, she'd be seen. Grace watched and waited and, within a few seconds, the car appeared around the corner.

It slowed down, then continued down the road and disappeared into the subdivision. Grace tried to get a glimpse of the driver, but the windows were too dark. She took out her cell phone and punched in Charles' number.

Grace told him what was happening, and he told her to go directly to his place. He'd meet her there in ten minutes.

Grace backed her car out of the parking lot and with her hands trembling, put the car in gear and went back the way she came. She then turned toward the highway instead of her original plan. If he was still following her, Grace could easily lose him on the QEW.

Joe pulled his car around the subdivision, but by the time he got back to where Grace was parked, she was gone. "Damn it," he swore. "The bitch got away from me. How could she have gone into the store and leave before I got back?"

He drove back the way he came in, but her car was nowhere to be seen.

She probably took the highway. Maybe she was on to me? He thought.

Joe checked his watch. "Damn it, I have to meet Sarah at the restaurant in ten minutes," he mumbled to himself. He pulled his car back toward Niagara Falls and headed back to Clifton Hill. He inched through traffic, turned right at the top of the Hill, and was at the restaurant in record time.

He cut the engine and sat in his car thinking. He'd been seeing Sarah a couple of weeks already, and she hadn't yet told him anything about the case. He was getting annoyed by this and was second guessing his decision to get involved with her.

His urges were becoming too overwhelming to ignore. He wanted to find another girl. He needed to find another girl. But with all his free time taken up with work and Sarah, he didn't have time to live out his fantasies. With the discovery of Jennifer, he didn't feel safe about kidnapping someone.

He was surprised that no one came knocking on his door to ask about Jennifer. They had a heated relationship for six months, and he was the last person to be with her before he accidently killed her, panicked then disposed of her body. It was then that he felt the rush and excitement.

It was the best sex he had with anyone when he took the cord and wrapped it around her throat. It was something they both had agreed upon. He'd lost all control as he tightened the cord around her neck.

He didn't pay attention as she scratched his back to try and break free. He didn't notice her turning blue and the life leaving her eyes. He didn't notice anything until he was finished. That was when the panic set in. He didn't know what to do.

Then he realized that no one knew about him. They were never seen together. She would come back to his place and stay the night or just a couple of hours. What they did together sexually was exciting as well as dangerous. When she died, he had to think of a place to put her body.

His house was already sold, and it was closing in a couple of weeks, so burying her in the yard would be stupid. Her body would definitely be found and traced back to him. He drove around for an hour until he came to a secluded area of the parkway.

The shore was treacherous, so there was no chance of anyone venturing there. Signs were posted along the railing warning people not to go past the barriers as they could easily be swept away by the currents. If it weren't for his smart thinking to tie a rope to a tree, then around his waist, he, too, would have been a victim of the Niagara River.

Once he put the body on the edge of the river, he took some large branches and leaves and carefully covered her completely. Even if someone did happen to come near that part of the railing, her body wouldn't be visible.

He left the body and hoped Mother Nature would do her job. With all the rain they had in the area lately, he thought for sure the river's edge would swell and sweep the body farther down river to Lake Ontario.

How could they have found it? How could anyone be able to see her unless they climbed the railing and was standing right there?

He had to know, and the only person he could ask would be Sarah. He knew he had to put his game plan into action tonight.

He was so deep in thought he didn't notice Sarah pull up beside him. She tapped on the window, startling him for a second. She smiled brightly as he got out of his car to greet her.

"You looked like you were in another world," she said, kissing him.

"Just thinking about work," he replied. "I'm starving. Let's eat."

The couple walked hand in hand into the Japanese restaurant and was seated in a secluded table away from prying eyes.

"How is work going?" Sarah asked. "With tourist season here, I bet you're busy."

"Yes. It's getting crazy down on Clifton Hill," he said. "I'm concerned, though, about this crazy guy running around killing people."

He wasted no time opening up the subject.

Sarah nodded. "I know what you mean. We have no more information now than we did a few weeks ago. I just wish we could find out who the boyfriend was."

He moved in closer. "Yeah, I understand. What I don't understand is how did you find the body? I mean, from what the news reports were saying it would have been pretty difficult to find unless you were looking for it."

Sarah rolled her eyes. "I guess I didn't tell you."

"Tell me what?" he asked nonchalantly.

"Grace found the body. Apparently she got one of her hocus pocus feelings and was led to the body."

"How the hell did she manage to find the body without falling into the water?"

She shrugged. "Beats me. I suppose she held onto the tree and saw a body part sticking out from underneath some branches and bush."

"And you believe that?"

"When it comes to Grace, nothing surprises me." She laughed.

Her date joined in. "Well, she was always a bit weird growing up."

"That's an understatement," Sarah added. "But seriously, it's just a matter of time until we find out who this boyfriend is. We're tracking her family now. We also found a phone number in some of her belongings."

The waiter poured two glasses of wine.

"The number's disconnected, but we'll be able to trace it to the previous owner," Sarah continued once the waiter left them alone.

He forgot about his number. He had it disconnected when he moved. It was in his mother's name, so he had to think of something in case they came asking.

"Are you thinking about work again?" Sarah asked.

He snapped out of his thoughts. "Oh, sorry. No, I was thinking about your case. It does sound strange. I just hope you can catch this guy before he kills again."

Sarah agreed. "Enough shop talk. Let's talk about us," she smiled.

They picked up their wine glasses to make a toast. "To us," she said as they clicked their glasses together.

"To us," he repeated.

Grace waited in her car until Charles arrived. The electronic gate shut behind him as he pulled his car next to hers.

Grace ran to his open arms as he got out of the car. "I've never been so scared," she cried.

He held Grace tight against him and kissed the top of her head. "It's okay. You're safe now. Are you sure you were being followed?"

Grace told him how the car slowed down as it passed her when she pulled into the store parking lot. "I'm positive."

"Would you recognize the car again if you saw it?"

"I'm not sure. It looked like every other car. Silver with dark windows."

"Dark windows? How dark?" he asked.

They moved their conversation inside the foyer of his house. "I don't know. They were really dark. The darkest I've ever seen."

"It might have been a custom job, but it would be nearly impossible to trace it. The car sounds generic to young people. They usually get custom tinting to spruce up their cars."

"I feel bad that I couldn't get a license number," Grace said.

"That's okay, baby. I just want you safe. We'll get the bastard."

Missy was tidying up the extra closet to make room for all of Jennifer's belongings. Her heart felt heavy knowing that she'd never come back for her things. Poor Jennifer, she thought. She spent all this money to have the costumes made and never got to wear most of them."

She pulled each costume out of the box, examining the detail of the pull away tabs.

Jennifer used to be a crude dancer until Missy was introduced to her.

She had taken Jennifer under her wing and taught her the art of being a stripper with class and dignity.

Jennifer changed her hair and makeup and started having beautiful costumes designed to make her look like a model.

Each costume represented a theme. Some were beauty queens, others played on customers' imaginations, such as the leather bondage outfit and the school girl costume. She would mostly wear the outfit that got her more tips. She even stole Missy's idea of a ballerina from the Nutcracker.

Although she couldn't stand on her toes like Missy could, she did the dance beautifully. Next to Missy, she was one of the best dancers, and made hoards of money.

Missy felt tears swell up and flow down her cheeks as she mourned over the loss of her friend. Jennifer never talked much about her family except that she was glad to be out from under their controlling ways.

But there was a dark side of Jennifer that Missy knew would be her demise. She prostituted herself. As much as Missy tried to convince her it was a dangerous way to live, she ignored it.

Missy knew she was a street walker before she became a dancer. She figured, since making the kind of money she was getting from dancing, she'd leave that dark world behind. But she didn't. The only difference was she took up with men from the club who were enchanted by her.

She became a high priced call girl on the side.

Missy lowered her head and wiped the tears from her face as she packed the rest of Jennifer's belongs and placed them on the empty shelf in the closet.

"Poor Jenny." She sighed. "Poor stupid Jenny."

She pulled out the card that Charles left and dialed the cell number. The voice mail came on. "This is Missy Maxwell. I need to talk to you in regard to Jennifer Smythe. If you could call me back as soon as possible, that would be great. I might have some information for you that could help," she said. She left the time of her call and her number before hanging up.

TWENTY-ONE

Grace and Charles were enjoying a quiet dinner together on the patio of his Victorian house. The evening weather had cooled only slightly but a breeze off the Niagara River allowed for a comfortable night.

They'd been seeing each other seriously for almost two months and spending every free moment together. With Grace spending more time at the house, the construction progress was going more smoothly. She was helping Charles by overseeing some of the work.

The interior designer that she suggested had some great ideas for the house. Because of Charles' workload, Grace was left in charge of approving all the designers' suggestions.

The landscaping design was another matter. Grace had no clue when it came to plants and was hesitant to approve anything. She drew the line on helping with that part of the renovation. Charles didn't mind her reluctance as he had a green thumb and loved to get his hands in the dirt.

They worked well together and because of this they enjoyed being with each other. But it's been difficult for them to find some alone time. Charles was knee deep in the murder case and Grace was busy with her work on Clifton Hill. Because of their erratic schedules they made each other a promise to try and spend the weekends together. So far they kept their promise.

It was past midnight when they decided to call it a night. Charles helped Grace put away the last of the clean dishes before they retired for the night. Grace glanced over at Charles as he wiped down the counter for her.

Grace was feeling domestic and she was actually enjoying it. She even found herself looking through cookbooks for recipes she'd like to try out. This was a whole new thing for her considering she hated to cook.

Grace crawled into bed next to Charles. He took his cell phone and flipped it on.

Grace looked at him with annoyance. "What are you doing? It's past midnight."

"I just want to check for messages before we go to sleep," he said.

"Even if you had messages, you can't call anyone back. It's too late," Grace said.

"Good point," he replied putting the phone on the night table beside the bed.

Charles flipped off the light and moved closer to Grace. His hands moved under her nightie and ended on her breasts.

"Are you in the mood?" he asked as his hands moved farther south.

"That would all depend," Grace said.

"Depend on what?"

"Whether it's going to be doggie sex or just plain sex," she replied.

"What's the difference?"

Grace thought for a moment. "About one hour and the length of time it takes for the soreness to go away the next day."

Before Charles had a chance to respond, his phone beeped with a message. "Hold that thought," he said as he turned on the light and dialed his voice mail. He took a pad and pen from the night drawer as he listened to the message from Missy. He wrote down her number and hung up the phone.

"Who was that?"

"Missy Maxwell. She said she might have some information about Jennifer." He dialed Sarah's cell and left a message for her to call him in the morning.

"Make sure you turn the phone off before you turn out the light." Grace insisted.

"Oh, now you're getting bossy," Charles replied as he flipped off the light.

"I just don't want any interruptions while we're having doggie sex," she whispered.

"Hmm, doggie sex. I like the sound of that," Charles said moving his hand back to her breasts then heading south.

Sarah and her ex snuggled beneath the down-filled comforter. The room was dark except for a few candles placed on the fireplace mantle. They had enjoyed a bubble bath together and had made love most of the evening. It was everything she had dreamt about.

She longed for this moment since high school, and now here she was, fulfilling her fantasy of making love to the man she carried a torch for since he first kissed her back in grade eight.

Joe lay next to Sarah with his eyes closed. He was bored and wanted the evening to end. He didn't want to draw suspicion by saying no when Sarah surprised him with her plans. Instead, he went along with it and faked almost every moment. Except for his orgasm, everything else was acted out.

She snuggled in closer, trying to entice him to perform again, but he wasn't in the mood. All he wanted to do was yank her by her hair and throw her across the room. But with his luck, she'd probably pull out her gun and demand a third time or she would shoot him. At this point he would choose the bullet. But he was in no mood to deal with that either.

"Look at the time," he said, glancing at his watch. "I better get going, baby."

Sarah sighed with disappointment. "I thought we could stay the night seeing that it's Sunday tomorrow."

"As much as I'd love to, I can't. Sundays are my busiest day and I need to open the café early." He grabbed his clothes and started to dress with his back turned to Sarah.

"Well, I might as well get going, too," she said as she pulled her naked body from the bed.

"Why don't you stay here? We're in separate cars. No reason you need to rush off. Enjoy the time alone," he urged her.

Sarah climbed back in the bed and wrapped herself in the warm blankets. "Maybe I will. I'm going to house hunt later today," she said as she grabbed her cell and flipped it on. "If you get bored later, you know where I am."

He gave her a smile and leaned in to kiss her just as her phone beeped a message. She pulled away and dialed her mailbox.

Listening intently, she jotted down the message and hung up. "So much for a day off." She sighed as she again pulled herself from the bed."

"What was that all about?"

"Do you remember Missy Maxwell?" Sarah asked.

"Yeah. Didn't she move to New York city to pursue dancing?"

"That's what I thought. It seems she's been dancing down at the same club as Jennifer Smythe."

"Was that Missy?" he asked, trying to look uninterested.

Sarah shook her head. "It was my partner. Missy left him a message to have him call her. She has some information that might help us with the case. He wants to meet me at the office in the morning."

Joe felt his heart race and he became lightheaded as he tried to keep his composure. "Was she a good friend of this girl?" he asked, trying to keep his voice calm.

"They worked together. Jennifer left some of her belongings at Missy's house. That's how we found the phone number. Anyway, I might as well go home and sleep. I can't show up at the office wearing the clothes I've got here."

Sarah said as she wrapped herself in the sheets.

"Maybe we can meet up after you finish work?" she asked.

Joe felt panic set in. He didn't want her to meet up with her partner. He didn't want her or her partner meeting up with Missy. But how could he stop her? How could he keep her from the meeting?

He took off his shirt and unzipped his pants.

"What are you doing?" Sarah asked. "I thought you had to go?"

"I can leave early in the morning to set up," he said pulling Sarah back in the bed beside him.

He kissed her deeply, holding her beneath him. Sarah felt his hands explore her body his mouth moved from her lips to her neck. He gently bit her neck, sending shivers through her body.

"I'm so glad you changed your mind," she whispered.

"So am I," he whispered back.

Grace opened her eyes to the smell of bacon and freshly brewed coffee. She stretched out her arms and yawned while focusing her eyes on her surroundings. She looked over at the alarm clock.

It was seven thirty and Charles was way ahead of her. He'd already showered and had breakfast prepared by the time Grace made her way down to the kitchen.

Charles handed her a cup of tea and went back to the bacon that was frying on the stove.

Grace watched him while she sipped her tea. She wasn't an early bird and hated to get out of bed before nine. Since she started sleeping at Charles' place she was lucky if she got to sleep past eight.

These early mornings were going to be the death of her if she didn't get at least one morning to sleep in.

"It's a good thing I love you," Grace said as she finished her tea. "All these early mornings and your cheery attitude can be a bit irritating."

Charles stopped what he was doing and turned to Grace. "You love me?"

Grace threw her head back slightly. "Out of all that I said, the only thing you got was I love you?"

"I got the rest of it too, but I choose to ignore it." He smiled and handed her a plate of bacon with two slices of whole wheat toast. "It's a well known fact that you aren't a morning person. Come to think of it, you're down right miserable before nine in the morning."

"That's because I'm normally asleep before then." Grace poured herself another tea and poured a coffee for Charles.

"So do you really love me?" he asked again.

Grace ran her fingers through Charles' wet hair and sat beside him. "Would it be a bad thing if I did?"

Charles shook his head. "Not a bad thing at all."

Grace leaned in and kissed him on the cheek. "Yes I do love you."

"I love you too," he said without hesitation.

This brought a smile to Grace's lips and a warm feeling in her heart.

Charles looked at his watch. "Want to have a quick one before I leave?"

Grace's eye widened. "You're joking right?"

"Nope. I never joke when it comes to sex."

"Should I remind you about last night and the hour of doggie sex we had?"

Charles leaned in and kissed Grace passionately. "It's forever etched in my mind as one of the best nights of my life."

"Once doggie sex is over the barn door is closed for awhile," Grace said.

Charles sat silently mulling over what Grace just said. "I have no clue what you just said but I'll take a stab at guessing that you're in no shape for any kind of sex at the moment."

"That's why you're a detective," Grace said with a smile.

Joe laid in bed listening to the sound of the shower. It was early and he convinced Sarah to shower before heading home. He was tired and spent the night lying awake worrying about the meeting with Missy.

Joe felt a rush of panic run through his body. What did Jennifer tell Missy? What did Missy know? What information does she have for the cops? So many questions, each one scarier than the other. He had to stop this meeting from happening.

He was deep in thought and didn't notice the bathroom door open.

"What's wrong?" Sarah asked as she walked into the room.

Her presence startled Joe. "What makes you think there's something wrong?" he asked.

"You just seem like a million miles away," she answered.

"I was just thinking that you haven't seen my new place yet," he said.

"You moved? When?"

"Quite a while ago. When my mother died, I sold the place and bought a couple of acres down the parkway."

Sarah sat on the bed beside Joe. She wrapped her hair up in a towel. "Sounds wonderful. I'd love to see it someday."

"How about now?" Joe suggested.

"Now? I can't. I have to get home and change before I meet up with my partner at the office."

Joe hooked two fingers on the front of the towel that Sarah had wrapped around her. He gently tugged on the towel, loosening it enough to expose her breasts.

"Oh come on. You're telling me you have to leave right now?" he asked kissing her breasts.

Sarah leaned back on the bed, pulling Joe on top of her. "Hmm, I suppose I could be a little late," she said as her breathing got heavier.

"Why don't you get dressed and follow me in your car?" he said. "We can continue this at my place."

Twenty minutes later Sarah was sitting in Joe's living room while Joe was in the kitchen making cappuccinos for breakfast.

"I know the place is a bit run down," Joe said. "Once I get it fixed up the place will be a jewel."

Sarah brushed some food crumbs from the sofa and made herself at home. "This place needs a good cleaning," she said as she looked around at the heaps of dirty laundry.

Dust bunnies had made their way out from under the furniture and settled in eye view in each of the corners of the room. Joe returned to the living room and handed Sarah a hot cup of cappuccino. He place a plate of store bought cookies on the table and joined her on the sofa.

"Sorry about the breakfast. I've been so busy at the café that I haven't had time to buy groceries." He apologized.

"That's okay sweetie. I usually just have coffee anyway," Sarah said as she sipped her drink.

Joe quietly watched Sarah out of the corner of his eye.

"How do you like the coffee?" he asked.

Sarah took another sip. "Yummy," she said with a smile.

She finished the cappuccino and gave out a yawn. "I guess I didn't get enough sleep last night."

Joe took the cup from Sarah and placed it on the table. "Do you want to lie down upstairs for a bit?"

Sarah shook her head. "I can't. I really have to get going."

She tried to stand but found herself frozen in her seat. "What's happening to me?" she cried as the room began to spin.

TWENTY-TWO

Charles checked his watch and called Sarah again. Her voice mail kicked in, so he left her another message.

He'd waited for over an hour for Sarah at the office but decided to leave without her.

"Sarah, where are you? I'm on my way to Missy's house, and I haven't heard from you yet. Call me as soon as you get this message."

He hung up and radioed into the station. "Can someone try calling Sarah's house to see if she's there? I can't seem to reach her on her cell."

"Ten-four. I'll have her call if I reach her," the operator replied.

Charles was feeling uneasy about this. It wasn't like Sarah to not call in. Even on her day off, she'd always call to touch base.

He arrived at Missy's place and parked in the driveway. He looked up and down the street hoping to see Sarah pull up any second, but the street was deserted.

He checked his watch again as the operator came on the radio telling Charles she had no luck reaching Sarah. "Her mother said she didn't come home last night."

"Okay, thanks," he said. Charles was beginning to get worried. He knew Sarah was a big girl and could take care of herself, but when someone does something out of the ordinary, his sixth sense kicks in.

He dialed Grace. "Hey, honey, it's me. I have a question for you. Do you know any guy Sarah might be seeing?"

He had no luck with Grace either. "If you hear anything, would you call me?"

Grace hung up the phone and finished cleaning the kitchen before heading back to her place. She wanted to talk with her mother and grandmother about Sarah's mother. She was a regular visitor to the store and if anyone knew anything about Sarah's personal life, she would. She was the towns' busy body and knew everyone's business.

By ten thirty Grace was sitting in her family's kitchen drinking a cold glass of lemonade. The day was hot and sticky, and every stitch of clothing clung to her like lint on a wool sweater.

"As far as Mrs. Child was concerned, Sarah wasn't seeing anyone," Mom said as she pulled up a chair beside Grace.

Granny was putting homemade cookies on a plate. She baked anytime of the year. Even if it was one hundred Fahrenheit in the shade she'd always have a fresh batch of cookies to share with customers and family.

"But then again, Sarah might not have told her mother everything. You know what her mother's like," Granny added.

The three women nodded and said yes in unison.

Grace took a bite of a cookie and thought for a moment. "What about an old boyfriend? Maybe she's with an old boyfriend?"

"She didn't have many boyfriends from what her mother said. According to Mrs. Child, Sarah was too busy focusing on school or her career to get involved with anyone," Mom replied.

"Or else the guy didn't want his relationship with Sarah spread around town," Granny said, referring to Mrs. Child's big mouth.

"True enough," they again said in unison.

"She's with someone," Grace said. "Someone she knows, but doesn't know."

"Do you think she met with foul play? Maybe the killer got her?" granny said.

That thought had occurred to Grace, but Sarah was too tough and too smart. If what granny was suggesting, could it be possible the killer is known to Sarah? Maybe they knew the killer, too? Maybe this person moved undetected among everyone?

"I think I'll go up to my apartment and try to contact Henry," Grace said, taking a few cookies with her. "Maybe the two of you can try a séance to find out anything new in the spirit world. We need to contact one of his victims."

Mom nodded. "We'll call Sarah's mother to help with the séance."

"Okay, but please don't tell her what we're suspecting. We don't want her to panic," Grace said before heading out the kitchen door and up the back stairs.

Sarah awoke and felt the pounding in her head. Her body hurt, and her vision was blurry, as she tried to focus on her surroundings. She didn't recognize the room and tried to remember what happened before she blacked out.

She tried to stand, but pain shot through her leg, and she cried out in agony. Her leg was broken, whether by accident or deliberate. The sound of a chain clanged against the floor as she moved her other leg.

She was shackled to something. "What the hell is this?" she whispered. "Where the hell am I?"

She looked around and found herself in a dingy bathroom that had seen better days. The smell of urine filled the air, and she felt her stomach heave.

"Hello?" she yelled. "What the hell is going on?" she yelled louder.

There was no response from the other side of the locked door.

She tried to pull herself to her feet again, but the pain was too great. She had no choice but to stay on the floor.

The last she remembered was having a cappuccino with Joe. After that, everything went black until she woke up on the floor.

Joe! She thought. Did he drug her? If he did, why would he do it? Another thought came to Sarah. A thought more terrifying. What if Joe was the serial killer and she was his next victim?

"Keep your head," Sarah said to herself. "You're a cop. You can subdue him."

How long was she out, and where the hell was she?

As much as she tried to control her emotions the fact is she was scared. A tear fell from her cheek as she cried in despair. She was truly afraid.

She knew her job was risky, and she was ready to die on the job. But she didn't want to die like this. She wanted to at the very least have a fighting chance. But with one broken leg and a shackle on the other, there was no chance for her. She wept uncontrollably praying for a miracle that would probably never come.

A sound came from beyond the locked door. Someone was coming. Panic shot through her, and she looked around the room for anything she could use as a weapon.

Before she had a chance to react, the door opened slightly. A tray was pushed across the floor toward her.

"Some food for you," the voice whispered. "Sorry about the leg. I have medicine for the pain," he added.

"What the hell are you doing Joe?" she demanded. "You know I'm a cop, and they'll be looking for me."

"Take the medicine and eat the food. You'll feel better," Joe said, ignoring her demands.

The door closed, and Sarah heard the lock click shut.

"If you let me go now, I'll make sure the courts go easy on you," she yelled.

She heard Joe leave the adjoining room and close the door behind.

She gritted her teeth and screamed under her voice. She was pissed. She was more determined than ever to get out of the situation she was in and kick the ass of her captor.

She picked up the sandwich, separated the bread, and sniffed the egg salad. She bit into the sandwich and washed it down with the large milk carton he supplied for her.

Sarah looked at the capsules and examined them. They read Extra Strength Tylenol on the side, so she popped two in her mouth and followed them with a gulp of milk.

She finished every bite of her meal and drank every drop of the milk when she started to feel dizzy. She sniffed the milk and realized it was drugged.

"Damn fucking damn!" she yelled as the room spun around her and her body became limp.

Missy greeted Charles at the door. "I'm sorry to drag you out on a Sunday but I felt this couldn't wait." She motioned for Charles to take a seat in the living room. Missy sat across from him in a rocking chair.

Charles pulled out a small tape recorder. "You don't mind if I record our conversation?" he asked. "I want to make sure I don't forget anything."

"Knock yourself out," Missy replied.

Charles flipped on the recorder, said his name, the date and time, and his location. "So what do you have for me?" he asked.

"I remembered something that Jennifer told me about her boyfriend," she said.

Love and Murder on the Hill

"Continue," Charles replied.

"At first I didn't think it was important, but when I was packing up her costumes, it hit me."

"What hit you?"

"She had her costumes made by her boyfriend's mother. That's how she met him."

"Do you know where she went for the costumes?"

"Sure do! When I was younger my mother would always have this woman make my ballet outfits. I told Jennifer about her when she started stripping."

"I hadn't seen this woman since I was younger. I never met her son because she was divorced and her ex-husband always had the son on weekends."

"Do you know where we could find her?" Charles asked.

Missy shook her head. "Unfortunately she died about a year ago."

"What about her son? Is he still around?"

Missy thought for a moment. "He inherited the house and his father's business. Last I heard he sold the house and moved away."

"So we're at a dead end." Charles sighed.

Missy smiled. "Not really. He never sold the business and I remember Jennifer telling me he ran a place on Clifton Hill."

"You wouldn't happen to know the name of the place or what he did there?"

"He was a bartender so it can't be too difficult to find out," she said. "How many places on Clifton Hill sell booze?"

"How many places on Clifton Hill sell booze where minors can go?" Charles added.

Charles changed the subject from Jennifer to Sarah. "I need to ask you something," he said.

"I don't know if I can answer you but go ahead."

"You were friends with Sarah Child."

Missy nodded. "We were friends in elementary school and for the first two years in high school."

"Why do you ask?"

Charles shrugged. "She's my partner and she was supposed to meet me here but I can't seem to find her."

"I gather this isn't normal behavior of Sarah's?"

"You got that right. Anyway, her mother said she had a date last night but never came home."

"You think she may be in trouble?"

"Let's hope not. I know it's a long shot but do you remember anyone she was ever interested in or dated when she was younger?"

"Sarah and I lost touch after grade ten. I went to New York to continue my education there. Before that Sarah never dated. At least not to my knowledge."

Charles turned off the recorder and placed it in his pocket. "Thanks for your help, Missy. If you can think of anything else in regards to Jennifer or Sarah please let me know."

Sarah awoke in small bedroom. She determined it was night and had been out for hours. Her leg was still shackled, but her broken leg had a makeshift splint, allowing for more movement and comfort.

The only window was boarded up from the outside, and the only furniture was the small bed that she was lying on as well as a wheel chair and a small table.

Based on her surroundings and the care taken to make sure she was comfortable, Joe was concerned for her well being. Beside the bed was an old service dolly. She must be on the second floor of the house, she thought, as she examined the ropes and pulley.

She tried to look down the shaft but it was dark except for a faint light coming from a crack at the bottom of the shaft.

There were two doors. One was closed and the other led to a small bathroom that hadn't been decorated since the early sixties. Green tiles surrounded the pink tub and covered the counter with a matching pink sink. Care was taken to ensure the bathroom was scrubbed clean.

He may be a kidnapper, but he's a clean one, Sarah thought. She maneuvered herself into the wheel chair and placed her broken leg on the raised part of the chair for comfort.

She slowly wheeled herself backwards into the bathroom.

The chain reached as far as the toilet, but wouldn't reach the bedroom door.

Fresh towels and toiletries were placed out for her use. She filled the sink with hot water and began to scrub herself from head to toe.

Her body still hurt, possibly due to being roughed up in her drug induced state. She brushed her teeth and washed her hair, wrapping it in a towel afterwards. There was a small window inside the tub area.

The glass was thick glaze, but the window was too small for her to fit through. Even if it were big enough, she was in no condition to be climbing through windows and shimmying down a roof.

The sound of a pulley being moved drew her attention away from the window. She moved herself back into the room just as a tray of food appeared in the service elevator.

Sarah took the tray and saw a shadow moving about at the bottom of the elevator. "What do you want from me?" she yelled down.

Joe ignored her and moved the trolley back down, closing the door behind him.

Sarah examined the size of the service elevator. She could fit nicely if it weren't for her broken leg. How convenient for him that her leg was broken. She was beginning to think that it was done on purpose to keep her from trying to get away.

She pulled the service elevator door down, slamming it shut, and swung her wheel chair around, cursing the whole time.

"Wait till I get my hands on you, you son of a bitch. I'll beat the shit out of you, and if there's anything left after I'm done, they can throw the rest in jail for life." She cursed.

TWENTY-THREE

The police were on full alert searching for Sarah. It had been two days since she disappeared, and they were no farther ahead in their search than they were the first day she disappeared.

Grace tried to focus on her work and did the best she could, but she was worried. Grace wouldn't say that Sarah and her were friends, but Grace knew her.

Grace didn't want anything to happen to her. She was a great cop, and she was Charles' partner. They watched each other's back, and her disappearance has affected him greatly.

He felt he should've protected her even though it wasn't his fault. Who would have thought she'd fall victim to anyone? Who would have thought that this serial killer would be so bold as to kidnap a cop, let alone a detective?

Grace took a break from work and decided to walk down Clifton Hill to clear her mind. Grace was a few stores down before she realized that Marco was beside her. He wrapped his arm around Grace, and it caught her off guard.

"I'm worried too," he said trying his best to comfort his friend.
"Why don't we go get Aaron and grab some lunch," he asked.
"Not hungry."
"How about a drink then?"
"Nope. Not thirsty."

Marco sighed. Grace turned and headed back up the Hill once she reached the parkway.

He turned and followed Grace back up. They walked in silence, but Grace could sense something on his mind.

"So what's up?" she asked as they turned the corner of the walk way.

He stopped at the corner as someone caught his eye, then grabbed Grace's arm, pulling her back on the Hill.

Grace pulled her arm free. "You're scaring me. What the hell is going on?"

"We need to talk," he said seriously. "I didn't want to say this in public but me and Aaron might have some information about Sarah's disappearance."

"If you know something, then you need to talk to the police."

"Can't do that. You know how I feel about cops. Besides, the last thing I need is cops sniffing around asking questions."

He looked over at his bell booth and Aaron's rock wall. A crowd was forming, and he needed to get back to work.

"We thought about something in regards to Sarah," he said looking around as if he were afraid someone would hear him.

"Okay. Let's meet at the Japanese place up the street tonight at nine," Grace said.

He gave out a sigh of relief. "Thanks. And please, no cops, okay? Just the Hardy Boys and Nancy Drew."

His remark made Grace smile.

He left Grace standing at the corner as he hurried back to his place on the walkway. She noticed him give Aaron a thumb up and Aaron gave Grace a nod as she returned to her table.

People were mingling around her table waiting for their turn. "Who's next?" Grace asked the crowd.

Missy was changing after her last set for the night. She was tired and a bit nauseous due to her early pregnancy. She decided to take a couple of days off to rest as she bid her boss and the other girls good night.

Stephen the bouncer offered to walk her to her car, but she declined. "Not too many people here tonight. I'll be fine," she said and disappeared into the night.

As she got closer to her car she beeped the doors unlock and slid into the driver's side. She turned the car on and checked herself in the rear view mirror. A hand reached up and pulled her head back while placing a cloth over her mouth and nose. She tried to fight, but he held her tight. She felt herself weaken, and then everything went black.

Once Joe was sure that Missy was out, he picked her up and put her in the trunk of her car. He drove her car to his house and took her body to the basement. He left her chained in the same bathroom where all his victims had been before.

He returned to Missy's car, drove it to her house, and parked it in her garage. He closed the garage and went inside the house to retrieve all of Jennifer's belongings. He carried the boxes out the door and to his car, which he had conveniently parked down the street earlier.

He was determined to not have Jennifer traced back to him. He hid his relationship with her from everyone but his mother. His mother had become aware of their relationship while designing and sewing the costumes for Jennifer.

If the cops were smart, they could have traced her costumes to him, but as of yet they didn't put two and two together.

He wanted to make sure they never did. His mother had passed on and so did his secret relationship with Jennifer.

Grace waited at the restaurant for Marco and Aaron. Checking her watch, she was beginning to get impatient. It was past ten, and they were already an hour late. Grace was about to leave when they walked in and came straight toward her.

Their smiles quickly disappeared at the disapproval look on Grace's face. "Sorry about that. It got really busy after you left and we didn't want to lose the business," Marco said apologetically.

"So what's this information you both have about Sarah?" Grace asked.

Marco ordered a beer. And Aaron ordered a coke. "You want something?"

Grace ordered a glass of white wine and some garlic bread to snack on.

They waited till the waiter was out of ear shot.

The three huddled together to discuss the missing detective.

"About a week ago I was walking the Hill and saw Sarah having lunch with someone on one of the benches," Marco said.

"Are you sure it was her?" Grace asked.

Marco nodded. "You can't mistake that red hair of hers. She looks like she belongs with the Summers family minus the ginger skin."

They all nodded in agreement.

"Anyway, she was looking pretty happy with him and that got me thinking about this nut who's been going around kidnapping tourists and killing them."

"What did you come up with?" Grace asked.

"As far as we know all the girls were under the legal drinking age, right?"

"Except for the most recent one, but they don't know if she was connected," Grace said.

"Okay, except for her. But all the others were under the drinking age," Marco said.

They all nodded.

"This guy isn't picking them up in a bar so it has to be a place where all ages could gather and feel comfortable. Some place where young girls would hang out with loud music," Marco added.

"Some place where he could go unnoticed while mingling with these women," Grace said.

Marco sat back in his chair. "Now you're getting the picture." He smiled.

"The Karaoke Café!" they said together.

Marco nodded. "The guy who Sarah was having lunch with was Smedley. He's run the place since his old man died. He'd have the perfect opportunity to meet women being the owner and all."

"Wait a second. Didn't Smedley and Sarah date for a brief time in high school?" Aaron asked.

"Yeah I think they did," Marco said. "In grade eleven they picked up for awhile. I don't think it lasted more than half a semester."

Grace felt a knot forming in her stomach. "We need to find Smedley and fast."

"Does anyone know his last name?" Aaron asked.

"Isn't it Smedley?" Grace said.

"I think his first name is Joe but I don't remember what his last name is," Marco said.

"I know who'd know," Grace said. "Missy Maxwell. She was Sarah's best friend in school. If anyone would know, she would."

Marco's mood changed. "Well you guys go on without me then."

Love and Murder on the Hill

Aaron and Grace stared at each other.

"We're the Hardy Boys. I can't do this without you," Aaron replied.

I'm the last person Missy would want to see right now," he said, lowering his head.

Grace instinctively put her arm around Marco. "What's going on? Want to talk about it?"

He shrugged. "I know you think I'm this macho man who sleeps with different women, but I'm not. I just like people to think so," he said.

"Okay so you're not a macho man whore. What's that got to do with Missy?" she asked.

"I was seeing Missy for about six months. I thought things were great and then one day she broke it off with me." His voice sounded hurt.

"I'm sorry to hear that. Did you try to contact her and ask her why?"

"Yeah, but she won't take my calls. So I went down to see her at work just after the reading you gave me. I thought maybe she might have given me some disease and that's why she didn't want to see me anymore."

"Did she talk to you?"

"No. So I went for a complete physical, and it came back clean."

Aaron tried to keep a straight face hearing about the reading Grace gave him.

"Were you pulling my leg with that reading?" he asked.

Grace smiled. "Oh, come on, Marco. What do you think?"

"I think you were saying those things to scare the shit out of me."

"Did it work?" Grace asked. "You're always hitting on me and that drives me crazy."

"Well, I can't say I didn't have it coming." He laughed." Besides, I haven't hit on you since we became private detectives."

"Just because Missy's an exotic dancer doesn't mean she sleeps around, "Grace said.

"If it's any consolation I may know the reason why Missy broke it off with you," Grace said.

"You know? Tell me!" Marco moved closer.

Aaron moved closer as well. "Hey I'm not going to be left out here," he said as Marco and Grace glanced at him.

"Okay I'll tell you but you have to swear on a stack of bibles you didn't hear it from me," Grace said.

Marco and Aaron put their right hand up and crossed their heart with their left.

"Missy's pregnant." Grace just blurted it out without giving it a second thought. "And I think you're the father."

The blood drained from Marco's face and he felt faint. Aaron grabbed his friend before he fell to the floor and Grace tried to help him drink some water.

"Are you okay buddy?" Aaron asked as he tried to steady his friend in his chair.

Marco took a couple gulps of water and asked for something stronger.

Grace switched the water for beer.

"Are you sure about this?" he asked.

Grace nodded. "Charles told me," she replied. "She also said that the father was a gigolo and she has no intentions of letting him be a part of the baby's life."

"Well, we'll see about that!" Marco said. "Check please!"

Fifteen minutes later the three of them were at Missy's door ringing the doorbell. They waited a few minutes and rang again.

Marco peered into the garage and spotted Missy's car. He rejoined his friends and rang the doorbell again.

"Maybe she's not home?" Grace said.

"She's home. Her car's here, so Missy's here."

He pulled out his keys and fumbled with them until he came to the right key and inserted it into the lock. "Missy gave me a key to her place, but forgot to ask for it back when she broke off with me."

He unlocked the front door, and they stood inside the dark entrance of her small bungalow.

"Missy? Are you here?" Marco called out. All the lights were off in her house, and there was no response.

That eerie feeling came over Grace again as if something was dreadfully wrong.

Marco flipped on the hall light and went straight to her bedroom. Her bed hadn't been slept in, and her kitchen had been cleaned.

"Is she always this neat?" Aaron asked.

Marco nodded. "She irons her towels."

Grace made a mental note not to ever let them in her apartment.

"She's usually home at this time. I'm worried."

Love and Murder on the Hill

"Maybe she went out with a friend?" Grace tried to reassure him but she wasn't too convincing. Grace knew something was wrong, and so did The Hardy Boys.

Grace pulled out her cell phone and punched in Charles' number. She told him of Missy's disappearance.

"Are you sure about this?" Charles asked.

"Dead sure," Grace replied.

"I'll be there in a few minutes," he said before hanging up.

They sat down to wait for Charles. "Do you know Jennifer?" Grace asked Marco, trying to make conversation.

He looked at her puzzled. "Jennifer? Who's Jennifer?"

"She was a friend of Missy's. They worked together."

Grace told Marco and Aaron about Jennifer and how she may have been the first victim of the serial killer who was running loose in Niagara Falls.

"I find it strange that Missy would associate herself with one of the dancers at the club, let alone one who used to prostitute."

"Maybe there's more to Missy than you know."

They were interrupted by the door bell. Marco jumped to get it, hoping it was some news about Missy.

Charles walked in and shook hands with Marco. "You must be Marco," he said, shaking his hand firmly.

Aaron stood and introduced himself. Charles nodded.

"Have you heard anything from Missy?" he asked as he greeted Grace with a kiss.

"Nothing yet. We're worried about her," Grace answered.

"I've been calling her cell but no answer," Marco said.

"Maybe there's a clue in her car?" Marco suggested.

They all shuffled into the garage and Marco flipped on the light.

The car was unlocked and Missy's purse was sitting on the passenger seat. A beeping sound came from inside the purse.

"That's her cell phone," Marco said.

He went to reach for it but Charles stopped him. "We need to have everything examined," he said. "Best not to touch anything until I get our guys in here to dust for prints."

They shuffled back into the living room and Charles dialed the office to get a crime unit in.

The all sat down to wait.

"What about this Jennifer person?" Marco asked.

"She left some of her belongings here. Maybe there's something I overlooked," Charles said.

They followed Marco into the spare room. "Missy keeps everything in this room that she's not using."

There were no boxes in sight, so Grace opened the closet door, but that too was empty. "Do you think she might have thrown out Jennifer's things knowing she wasn't coming back for them?" Aaron asked.

Charles shook his head. "I doubt that. She knew we might need them, and she did say she and Jennifer shared dance outfits. She may have tucked them away in her own possessions."

"Missy made her own costumes," Marco said. "She may have done just that seeing that there's no one else in the area who can make the costumes anymore."

"What do you mean?" Charles asked.

"I remember Missy telling me about the woman who made costumes for all her ballet recitals. She used to make all the costumes for the dancers at the club. Apparently she died recently and that's why Missy made her own costumes." Marco said.

"Do you know who was making the costumes?" Grace asked.

"I know who," Aaron said. "Emma took ballet with Missy when they were young. This lady made all the costumes. She's the best."

"Was the last name Smedley?" Charles asked.

The three looked at each other.

"That was his last name after all," Grace said.

"Who's name?" Charles asked.

They were interrupted by a knock at the door and everyone jumped. Charles went to the door and opened it to the crime unit. He filled everyone in on what he had so far and the guys went to work, starting with the garage.

Police lights in the driveway brought out the neighbors and Charles instructed two uniformed officers to cordon off the property.

Charles rejoined the trio in the living room. "You want to tell me what you were talking about before we were interrupted?"

"Joe Smedley's mother used to sew the costumes for Missy when she was taking ballet," Grace said.

Sarah and Joe dated for a little while in high school." Marco added.

"Do you know where we can find Joe Smedley?" Charles asked.

"He runs the karaoke bar on Clifton Hill," Grace said.

Charles rubbed his forehead as he felt a headache coming on from stress. "I want you three to go to Grace's apartment and stay there until you hear from me." Charles ordered.

"We can't just sit there and wait," Grace said. "We need to find Missy and Sarah."

"Let me do my job. We'll find them."

"But Missy's carrying my baby. I need to help her." Marco demanded.

"You're the father?" Charles asked.

Marco nodded. "Yeah and she needs to be found now!"

"You can do us all a favor and take Grace home and wait there. I want you both to look after Grace for me," Charles said. "That's what you can do to help."

Against their better judgment, the three of them climbed into Grace's car.

Charles leaned into the driver's window and kissed Grace on the lips. "Go straight home, hear me?"

"Yeah, we'll go straight home," Aaron said from the back seat.

"The café is closing soon and Joe Smedley will be closing up. I'll go there and have a talk with him," Charles said.

"That's a great idea," Grace said. "Get there before he leaves."

TWENTY-FOUR

Grace backed out of the driveway, put the car in drive and headed back to the highway.

"We can't go back to your place," Marco said. "There's no way I can sit around knowing that Smedley has my Missy."

"We can't go to the bar. Charles will freak out if he sees us there." Grace said.

"Does anyone know where Smedley moved to when he sold his mothers place?" Marco asked.

"No but I might be able to find out." Aaron pulled out his cell and dialed his mother.

After several rings she answered. "Mom can you open up the office for us? We need your help," he said. After an exchange of words, Aaron hung up the phone.

"What's that all about?" Grace asked.

"Head down to Dorchester. My mother's going to meet us at her real estate office," Aaron said. "If anyone can find his new address she can."

Marco gave his friend a high five and Grace whipped the car around heading towards Dorchester Road.

Dorchester Road consisted mostly of houses and small businesses. The closer you got to the highway the more commercial it became with larger store chains and shopping malls.

They pulled into a strip mall that housed a local real estate office as well as an asian nail salon, variety store and a Tim Hortons.

They parked in front of the real estate office with the car doors locked and the engine running, until Madeline Stein pulled alongside them.

Grace cut the engine and the trio piled out of the car.

"This better be good," she said to Aaron. "You know how I hate to be dragged out of bed in the middle of the night."

Madeline unlocked the door, turned off the alarm and flipped on the back room lights. "Now what's so damn important that it couldn't wait till morning?" she asked as they went to her personal office?

She sat at her desk and motioned for everyone to take a seat, while she turned on her computer.

"Do you remember when Mrs. Smedley died?" Aaron asked.

"Sure do. We got the listing from her son to sell the house."

"Do you recall if her son bought another place?" Grace asked.

Madeline thought for a moment. "If he did, our office didn't represent him." Aaron moved around the desk and stood behind his mother, looking over her shoulder. "Is there any way you can find out?"

"I can cross reference anything sold around the same time as his mothers place," she said. "If he bought something it would show his name."

She punched in a few commands on the computer and narrowed the search to thirty days after the sale. A listing of over fifty houses came up. "I'll print out four copies so we can go through them."

She went to another room and returned a few minutes later with copies of the listings.

They looked over the listings but none had Joe Smedley's name as purchaser.

"Is it possible he could've bought under another name?" Grace asked.

"Anything's possible," Madeline said. "There's two here that were bought by numbered companies. One of them could be his."

"How can we find out?" Grace asked.

"Let me trying something," Madeline said. She punched in a few more commands and a listing came up on the screen. She took the printed list with the two numbered companies and compared them with the listing on her screen. "Bingo!" she said.

The trio moved around the desk to look at the screen. "That's the café that Joe's father left him," Aaron said.

Madeline nodded. "His father bought the property years ago. I wasn't sure if he still owned it but if he did he'd have his name on the deed."

"Seems the old man was smart enough to put it in a numbered company to protect his personal assets." Madeline continued.

"Joe must have known and used the company to purchase the new property," Aaron said.

He kissed his mother on the cheek and thanked her.

"You don't need anything else?" she asked.

"Nope. We've got all we need," Aaron said, taking the address with him.

They climbed back into Grace's car and waited until Aaron's mother locked up and went home.

"What do we do now?" Grace asked.

"We go down to Joe's house and kick some Smedley butt!" Marco demanded.

"You know Charles will kill us?" Grace said.

"We don't tell him," Aaron replied. "Besides, we're just going to take a look."

Grace blew out a sigh, put the car in gear and headed towards the parkway.

They arrived at the entrance to Joe's property. Grace pulled the car to the side of the road and cut the engine.

"We need a plan," she said. "We can't just go in there with guns a blazing."

"I can," Marco said as he opened the car door.

Aaron grabbed him by the collar and pulled his friend back into the car. "Grace is right. We need to have a plan."

An idea came to Grace and she made a call on her cell.

"Who you calling?" Marco asked.

"The Summers twins," Grace replied. "We could use their help."

After a brief conversation and an exchange of words, Grace hung up. "Let's go," she said starting the engine. "The twins will be waiting for us at the end of their street."

Ten minutes later they found themselves driving slowly down the street where the Summers family lived. "They should be here somewhere," Grace said as they combed the deserted street for movement.

Two silhouettes appeared from behind a tree just as Grace passed. They waved the car down and Grace pulled over to the curb.

"What's happening!" Ricky said sticking his head in the driver's window.

Robby tapped on the trunk and Grace popped the lid. He put two black duffle bags in the trunk and slammed it closed.

"Let's roll," Robby said as the twins climbed in the back seat.

The twins were dressed in night gear from head to toe. They had black toques on their heads covering the red hair and ginger faces.

"Great getups," Aaron said. "We need something like that."

"We're on it man," replied Ricky. "We have night gear for everyone including our lady driver."

The twins made some hand slapping handshake.

"I'm Nancy Drew," Grace said.

"And we're the Hardy Boys." Marco joined in.

The twins looked at each other and shrugged.

"Whatever floats your boat man," Robby said.

They returned to the driveway, cut the engine and they all piled out of the car. Grace popped the trunk and the twins removed the duffle bag. They quietly closed the trunk as not to alert anyone of their presence.

"So what's the plan?" Marco asked as Ricky passed out black clothing.

"Hey dude, I though you guys had a plan," Robby said as he pulled his toque over his face.

"I need to call Charles," Grace said dialing his number.

Marco grabbed the phone from her. "Let's wait until we survey the area. If we can't rescue Sarah and Missy ourselves, then we'll call him," he said handing the phone back to Grace.

"I thought we were just going to look?"

"Yeah, we're gonna look and then we're gonna kick ass."

Grace sighed. "No one told me anything about ass kicking."

She couldn't recall reading if Nancy Drew or the Hardy Boys ever kicked ass in any of their adventures. As a matter of fact, she couldn't remember the word ass being used at all.

They dressed themselves in the clothes the twins brought for them and pulled the black toques over their faces. The five of them walked along the road that led to Joe's house. The driveway was surrounded by overgrown bush and mature pine trees. The farther they travelled the darker it became.

Ricky pulled out a penlight and shone it on the ground.

"Better not use the light bro," Robby said. "We're making a surprise attack and the light will tell the enemy our whereabouts."

Ricky flicked off the light and the group slowly made their up the dark road.

A light flickered through the trees as they turned the corner and came to a clearing. In the distance stood a weathered cottage.

"What a dump," Aaron whispered.

"Yeah but look at the property," Marco said.

The house was worthless but the land was prime real-estate. The cottage sat on three acres of parkway greenery.

The group moved themselves towards the pine trees and huddled together.

"We still need a plan." Grace once again reminded the group.

"Already on it," Ricky said as he pulled out a small tool pouch. "I'm gonna go hot wire his car and Robby's gonna shimmy up the drain pipe to enter through the second floor.

Grace, you go round back and when you hear Joe come out, you go through the back door and hide in the basement. Marco and Aaron, you guys go through the front door and slam it shut. Find something to barricade the door so he can't get back in."

It sounded like a great plan and in theory it would probably work. The only flaw in the plan was Grace was shaking in her boots and wanted to throw up. Aaron and Marco were trying to put on a brave front but were rethinking their part in all this.

"What if he's got a gun?" Aaron asked. "I don't want to get shot. Emma would be pretty pissed if I get shot and I die. All the money she's put out for our wedding isn't refundable."

Ricky made a grunting sound and threw his hands in the air. "What are you guys, amateurs?"

The trio nodded.

"Okay plan B," Ricky said.

Robby opened the other bag and pulled out three paintball guns that were loaded them with pellets. "Anyone play paintball before?" he asked.

Aaron reluctantly raised his hand and Robby handed him a gun.

"I never knew you went paintballing," Marco whispered to his friend.

"Went once with Emma's family for her little brothers' birthday party," he replied.

"How'd that work out for you?" Marco asked.

Aaron shook his head without answering.

"Oh, that bad," Marco said. "We're screwed then."

"Let's hope they've got a plan C." Aaron whispered.

"So this is the new plan," Robby said. "I'll hotwire the car and Marco, you drive it away. When the killer dude comes out, Ricky and I and our man Aaron will hit him hard and fast with paint pellets.

"What do I do?" Grace asked raising her hand.

"You're gonna sneak in the back door and hide in the basement."

"So basically the same thing as plan A," she replied. "Why do I have to hide inside?"

"Because we're gonna be too busy distracting him," Ricky replied. "Besides, if the serial killer dude has a gun, we don't want you to get shot."

"Good point," Grace said.

Once they had their parts memorized they regrouped and slowly moved closer to the house. A silver car with dark windows sat at the end of the drive and Grace immediately recognized the car as the one which followed her down the parkway.

She felt a knot form in her stomach as she moved around the side of the house. Aaron kept pace with her to make sure the back was clear for her to hide and wait.

The back door was open except for the screen door. Hmm, she thought. That's easy access.

A light was on in the kitchen and Grace stretched her neck to see inside.

The kitchen looked as if it'd been through the war. The appliances were new but the décor screamed fifties. Trays with dirty dishes were stacked up on the counter.

Grace sized up the distance from the back door to the basement, to the living room. About ten feet total.

Aaron motioned for Grace to hide in the bushes and wait for the signal. Grace crouched down out of sight and Aaron sprinted back around the house to join the rest of the group.

"All set," he said as he stood next to Ricky who was standing guard.

Robby had popped the lock on the car and was in the process of hotwiring it.

Marco sat in the driver's side ready to put it in gear when the engine started. "What's taking so long," he asked impatiently.

"Chill dude. I'm working in the dark here," Robby said.

Seconds later the engine kicked in and Robby jumped from the car. Marco wheeled the car around and tore down the driveway leaving the others in a dust cloud.

"Get ready man," Ricky said to Aaron as a shadow crossed the window on the main floor.

The front door flew open and Joe hit the porch running, taking two steps at a time, ending up on the lawn. "What the fuck?" he screamed as he saw his car disappear up the drive.

He was too much in shock to notice Aaron and the twins standing at the edge of the porch.

"That's for taking our club house you bastard!" Ricky yelled as he fired off round after round of blue paint pellets.

"Yeah dude! We're taking the car in retaliation for you taking our club house!" Robby said, as he let Joe have it with pink pellets.

Aaron was shooting yellow in every direction. He hit the trees, the front of the house and everything in between, except the intended target.

It didn't help with the fact that he'd closed his eyes the moment he pulled the trigger.

Joe hit the dirt and made a belly crawl towards the porch as he was hit from all sides by the twins.

Grace heard the commotion in the front yard and darted from her hiding place. She hit the steps to the back door and within seconds, was standing inside the kitchen. She moved towards the basement door, opened it and stepped into total darkness. She took out the small penlight Ricky gave her and flipped it on as she closed the basement door.

Grace hurried down the stairs and hid behind some boxes under the stairs. She could still hear the sound of paintballs hitting the house and Joe swearing up a storm as Grace tried to adjust to her surroundings. A few moments later the front door slammed shut and the sound of footsteps followed.

Joe had locked the front door and went to dial the police but stopped short. "What the fuck am I doing?" he said out loud. "I can't have the cops snooping around here." He hung up the phone and went back to the living room.

He turned off the lights and peeked out the living room window. It was splattered with paint, mostly yellow, making it difficult to see movement outside. "Two can play at this game," he said as he went to the hall closet and retrieved his pellet gun.

He moved back to the kitchen, found the container of pellets and began to load his gun. The twins had positioned themselves near the back door while leaving Aaron to man the front. They glanced in through the screen and saw Joe loading his pellet gun.

Without warning they fired off several rounds of pink and blue paint right through the screen door, catching Joe by surprise.

"Eat paint, you son of a bitch!" yelled Ricky as he fired off another five pellets.

The screen from the door ripped down the center as paint filled the kitchen.

Joe turned his pellet gun and fired off a few rounds through the hole in the screen door.

"I'll get you, you little fuckers!" he screamed as he flew through the back door and into the night.

The twins separated and headed for cover as Joe fired blindly in all directions.

Grace looked around the room for any signs of life. The room smelled damp and moldy and the hairs on the back of her neck stood up. She felt death around her. Something terrible had happened in this basement, she thought.

Grace wandered around looking for any sign of the two women. The basement had a makeshift rec room with a low ceiling.

A lone couch with a nineteen sixties style coffee table sat in the middle of the room. There was no other furniture. No pictures on the walls, no television set, no wet bar with tacky pine paneling.

She wished there was a bar down there. She was shaking like a leaf and could use a stiff drink right about now.

A closed door sat on the other side of the room. Grace quietly slid out from her hiding place behind the stairs and moved towards the door.

Grace opened the door, and the smell of death filled her senses. In the middle of the room was a table that had makeshift braces at each corner. It reminded Grace of some medieval torture device she'd seen at one of the horror museums on the Hill.

Grace rubbed my fingers along the table and examined the red stains. She felt her heart race as she realized the stains were dried blood. Grace's head buzzed with fear as she searched for another door. There had to be another one, she thought.

The walls were lined with thick paneling. The only door Grace found was the one she'd entered through.

Maybe there's a hidden door, Grace thought as she ran her hands along the walls, pushing every foot or so in hope that something would spring open.

Grace was near the far end of the third wall when she heard a click. The wall moved open, exposing a dingy bathroom. Grace felt for a light switch, found it, and flipped it on.

Grace gasped at the sight of Missy gagged and shackled to the pipes under the sink. Her eyes were wide and swollen from crying.

Grace pulled the gag from her mouth and shushed her to keep quiet as she examined the chain.

"Someone abducted me," she cried. "I didn't see who it was. How did you find me?"

"Missy, you need to be quiet. Joe Smedley kidnapped you."

"Smedley? Why would he do this? What does he want with me?"

"I'll explain later. In the meantime we need to get you out of here." Grace pulled out her cell phone. No signal. "Damn it. Why the hell can't I get a signal?"

Grace turned her attention back to Missy. "Missy, you need to be quiet. I need a key to unlock this chain. I have to leave you here so I can try to call for help on my cell." She nodded in agreement. "How did you get here without him seeing you?" she asked.

"I had some help. Some friends created a diversion so I could slip in the house and search for you and Sarah."

"He has Sarah too?"

Grace said. "We think so, but for now you have to be very quiet while I'm gone."
Grace moved through to the other room. Still no signal. She moved around the basement until she was standing at the bottom of the stairs. It was no use. She couldn't get a signal anywhere in the basement.
She looked up the stairs and listened for sounds of life. All was quiet. She moved back to the bathroom where Missy was. "I can't get a signal down here," Grace said. "I need go back upstairs."
Missy began to cry. "Please don't leave me Grace." She begged.
"I promise I won't be long," Grace said. "I need to turn the light out in case Joe comes down here while I'm gone."
Missy nodded. "Please hurry."
Grace gave her a hug. "I'll be back soon."
Grace turned off the light, leaving Missy in the dark. She closed the door and quietly slipped through the other door until she was standing the rec room.

She once again moved to the bottom of the stairs listening for any movement above. The door opened and Grace slid behind the stairs.
The room filled with light as Joe moved down the stairs. He stood in the rec room scanning the area for anything unusual. "Fucking kids," he mumbled as he moved to the other side of the room and disappeared through the door.
Grace's heart was pounding in her ears and the knot that was in her stomach had graduated to a heavy rock. She wanted to throw up but decided to wait till she was outside. She slowly moved from her hiding spot and sprinted up the stairs, taking two at a time.
Grace was nearly at the top when she felt a hand grab her leg. She lost her balance as the hand pulled Grace back down the basement stairs. Without thinking, Grace whirled her body around with her leg still held, and brought her other foot up making contact with Joe's chin.

The force of Grace's kick knocked him down the stairs and across the room. Grace scrambled to her feet, and was back on the stairs when she felt the pain go through her leg.
She screamed out in agony, as she moved up the stairs. Grace grabbed her leg and realized there was a metal object protruding just above the knee.

Joe had somehow managed to stab her with a knife before she kicked him across the room. Grace took a deep breath and tried to pull the knife out but the pain was too excruciating.

Grace turned and headed back up the stairs just as Joe regained his composure and ran after her. He reached out to grab her but missed.

Grace managed to make it through the door and slammed it shut.

"Ricky, Robby, Aaron," Grace screamed as she limped through the back door and fell down the steps.

Aaron rushed to Grace's side, lifted her in his arms and carried her away from the house. He hid her in the pine trees just as Marco appeared down the driveway carrying a baseball bat.

"Where's the twins?" Grace asked as Aaron examined her wound.

Aaron pointed to the house just as the twins were positioning themselves on the roof. One was trying to look in the boarded up windows while the other stood guard.

It was hard to tell which was which because they were dressed alike.

"They're like friggin monkeys," Aaron said. "They shimmied up the drain pipe like there's no tomorrow."

"I found Missy," Grace said.

"Where is she?" Marco asked half hysterical.

"She's in the basement. She's okay. Just scared," Grace said. She took out her phone and punched in Charles' number.

"Grace? Where are you? I've been trying to call you for the past half hour," Charles asked.

"Promise you won't get mad?" Grace asked.

Charles went silent for a moment. "You didn't go home did you?"

"Well not exactly," she said trying to calm herself even though she was in pain.

More silence.

Grace listened and for a moment. She thought she heard Charles counting to ten. "We found Missy," Grace said before she fainted.

Aaron took the phone. "Charles, Grace is hurt. We need an ambulance and we need lots of cops." He proceeded to give Charles the address and quickly hung up the phone.

TWENTY-FIVE

Charles felt a knot form in his stomach at the thought of Grace laying hurt in the woods. He called head quarters and arranged for a swat team to surround the house.

Joe appeared at the door holding Missy. He had one arm wrapped tightly around her chest, holding her close to him as protection. In his other hand he held a knife to her throat and threatened to kill her if his car wasn't brought back to him.

"Fuck this shit!" Marco yelled, and headed in Joe's direction carrying the bat. He stopped in his tracks as he saw the knife at Missy's throat.

"I'll cut her Marco. I mean it. Get me my car and let me go and I'll let her go," Joe demanded.

The Summers twins moved quietly across the roof to the front of the house. Marco glanced up slightly and saw the twins taking position behind Joe.

Joe's adrenalin was pumping fast as he moved slowly down the front steps. "Where's my car?" he screamed at Marco.

"I'll get it for you. Just don't hurt Missy." Marco begged.

He jogged down the road and returned a few minutes later with Joe's car. He parked close to Joe and stepped out of the car.

"Back off!" Joe ordered Marco as he moved closer to the car.

The sound of police sirens were in the background. Joe freaked as he backed towards the car holding Missy in front of him. He pushed her out of the way just as he slid into the driver's seat.

The Summers twins sent a barrage of paint balls at the car, as Marco grabbed Missy and the two ran for cover.

They pelted the front windshield until there wasn't a clear space to see out of.

Joe hit the gas and blindly drove into a maple tree. The airbag inflated as the hood crumpled in a V shaped.

Marco ran to the driver's side and yanked the door open.

He grabbed Joe by the collar and dragged him out of the car before Joe had a chance to gather his thoughts and react.

Marco pulled back and punched Joe right in the face, knocking him to the ground and out for the count.

"Kidnap my girlfriend will you?" Marco said as he gave Joe a kick while he lay on the ground.

Missy ran to Marco's side. "My hero!" she cried as she threw her arms around him and kissed him passionately.

The Summers twins high fived each other before climbing off the roof and hiding their paintball guns.

They made their way over to where Aaron and Grace were.

"If anyone asks, the guns belong to Marco," Ricky said.

Aaron chose not to question them and went back to Grace who was coming around.

Within five minutes the driveway filled with cruisers as Charles cuffed Joe and handed him over to a uniformed police officer. Two paramedics were attending to Grace in the back of an ambulance, while two others were taking Sarah on a gurney to another ambulance.

Missy refused to go by ambulance to the hospital but agreed to let Marco take her. Aaron and the twins were giving statements to the police when Charles came over to the ambulance where Grace was being treated.

"How's she doing?" he asked the attending medic.

"She'll live. We got the knife out and no major arteries were cut. A few stitches and some bed rest and she'll be good as new," he replied.

"Can I have a few minutes alone with her?" Charles asked as he climbed in the back of the ambulance.

The medic nodded and climbed out to allow some privacy for Charles and Grace.

"I guess you're mad," Grace said lowering her eyes.

"That's an understatement," he answered. "You could've got yourself killed."

"But I didn't." Grace smiled.

"But you could've."

"But I didn't."

Charles rubbed his forehead and silently counted to ten again. "I see this is hopeless." He leaned over and kissed her.

Grace felt a rush of warmth run through her body as his lips touched hers.

They were interrupted by the medic. "We need to get her to the hospital," he said climbing in the back.

Charles climbed out to allow the medic to do his job. "I'll be at the hospital later."

"What about Sarah? Did you find Sarah?" Grace asked.

Charles nodded. "She's got a broken leg, but she's fine."

Grace laid back on the gurney. "Thank God," she whispered as tears of relief fell from her eyes.

Charles threw her a kiss, closed the doors and watched as the ambulance disappeared down the drive.

Grace was recuperating by the pool when Missy appeared through the French doors of the sunroom with Charles beside her.

It had been a month since Joe was captured, and he admitted to everything, including the murders of Becky, Jennifer, and the other bodies that were found.

The wound on Grace's leg was deeper than first thought, and as soon as it heals, she'd have to endure several weeks of therapy to regain proper movement.

Sarah was on sick leave from the force until her leg healed. They had to re-break it and set it properly using pins, and she, too would have weeks of therapy to look forward to.

Missy and Marco rekindled their relationship and he asked for her hand in marriage, which she quickly answered yes. To Missy's surprise and everyone else's Marco had been saving the money he made from the business he shared with Aaron.

He invested a lot of the money in real estate and owned a large building that he agreed to turn into a dance studio for Missy. Ricky and Robby became overnight celebrities with their paintball friends. They even managed to get themselves girlfriends who were into paintballing as well.

Their parents gave them back their paint ball guns under the condition that they were only to be used at the paint ball arena. They agreed and all was right in the cosmos for them and everyone else.

Except for Grace who was feeling a bit blue and down in the mouth. She was bored sitting around all day and not working. She wasn't able to go back to her own apartment because of the stairs, so she had to be satisfied with staying at Charles' house.

It was either that, or staying with her mother and grandmother. That would have sent Grace over the edge within a couple of days.

Work was being done on the house around her, and Charles hired a neighbor's daughter to babysit Grace while he was at work. She felt totally useless.

Grace couldn't even go for a swim because of the wound on her leg. All she could do was sit around and read or watch television.

Missy hugged Grace, and Charles pulled a chair over for her to use.

"How are you feeling?" Grace asked as Missy sat down next to her.

"Aside from some morning sickness, I feel fantastic. My life couldn't be any better." She laughed with delight. "Marco's moving in with me next month."

"Sounds like you and Marco are going to have a great life together." Grace smiled.

She leaned back to let the sun warm her face. "I've never been so happy. Who would have thought that Marco, the man whore of Niagara Falls, would be the man of my dreams?" she laughed.

Grace laughed along with her. "So what brings you out here today?" Grace asked.

"I came to ask you something." Her voice turned serious.

Charles excused himself allowing them to talk in private.

"Sure, Missy. What can we do for you?" Grace asked.

"Our baby is due at the end of the year, and I talked this over with Marco. He and I both agree that we'd be honored to have you be the godmother."

"You don't have to answer right away," Missy said. "Just think about it."

Grace shook her head and reach out to her new friend. "There's nothing to think about. I'd be honored," Grace said, hugging Missy.

Missy took a deep breath and exhaled. "Thank you so much. We weren't sure if you'd want to, seeing that you don't know me very well, and in the past I wasn't that nice to you."

"The past is the past. Let's look at this new baby as a new beginning for everyone," Grace said.

"I'm going to tell Marco the good news," she said, getting to her feet and hugging Grace tightly. "Thank you so much, Grace. You're a wonderful friend and a great human being."

Missy hurried across the lawn towards the driveway. Grace watched as she made her way around the side of the house and to her car.

Charles rejoined Grace in the garden. "Missy's gone already?" he asked.

Grace nodded. "She wants me to be the godmother to her baby." Grace beamed.

He picked Grace up in his arms and carried her toward the house. "I think they made the right choice," he whispered.

Grace kissed him on the cheek and wrapped her arms tightly around him as he carried her through the sunroom doors.

"I love my time here with you Charles, but I've been here too long. I really should go back to my home."

He carried Grace up the stairs and into the master bedroom, laying her on the cool white sheets and placing a pillow under her bandaged leg. "My sweet amazing Grace, you are home."